A SOLDIER'S PROTECTION

BEYOND VALOR 4

LYNNE ST. JAMES

A Soldier's Protection

 Created with Vellum

A SOLDIER'S PROTECTION

He lost her once. Now he has a second chance. All he has to do is keep her alive.

Ex-SEAL Chase "Frost" Brennan was sure he'd never again see the only woman he'd ever loved. Faith Murdock was the civilian psychologist who'd brought him back to life three years ago, and now she was a seductive, alluring, burlesque dancer who'd hypnotized him. She had a story to tell, but before he could ask, all hell broke loose at the club.

Faith started dancing for release but when her fan mail turned threatening, it terrified her. When Chase showed up her relief was staggering. He was the one man she trusted with her life. She'd never gotten over the pain of having to push him away for his own good, even though it broke her heart.

Faith wasn't the same woman he'd known, and Chase wanted to know why. He was determined to break down the barriers to her heart, but first he had to catch a killer and it quickly became clear he was no ordinary stalker. Even with the help of his ESP team and his best friend, Chase would have to put his life on the line for his woman. But he was willing to do anything to give Faith the happily ever after she deserved.

To those who serve, the families they leave behind, and those who make the ultimate sacrifice.

Home.

 It'd been over three years since Chase "Frost" Brennan, former Navy SEAL, stepped foot in Coronado, so the feeling of being back where he belonged was the last thing he expected. For over fifteen years it had been home and the base for countless missions with his team. They'd been through hell and back more times than he could remember, and afterward they'd always met for a drink at CC's Saloon. Until that last mission, the one that ended his career. It was still a punch in the gut. Every moment permanently etched in his brain.

 It had been the mother of all clusterfucks.

Plan A turned into Plan F. He and Riot were the only survivors, and it had been touch and go for Riot. Though Chase had taken several shots, he carried each of his men to the rendezvous point. No one was left behind. Survivor's remorse permeated his every waking moment, he should have been the one to die that day. He'd wanted to die, but he'd been rescued by a tiny spitfire who wouldn't take no for an answer. She'd awakened feelings he'd forgotten, but then he'd lost her too.

Turning off the ignition of his rental car, he gazed at the front door of the club that had been his 'hangout' for years. Memories flooded his mind as the walls he'd erected tumbled down. "Fuck." Maybe coming back hadn't been the best idea.

It was the past. His old life, one that didn't matter anymore. When he left, he cut all the ties with everyone that had been part of this life as an operator. Okay, that was a lie. He'd had his computer whiz, Rock, keep track of Riot and Faith. The kid had to wonder why but he'd never asked.

Willow Haven, Florida was where he was

born and raised and after leaving California it was the obvious place to start over. After a few months, he'd put together a team and opened the Eagle Security & Protection Agency—ESP for short, and he liked short. It was his baby, and he was damn proud of what they'd accomplished. Soon medically retired ex-Ranger, Alex Barrett would be part of the team, and then they'd be able to expand their scope of operations. The man had crazy computer skills almost rivaling Rock's, but he wouldn't be the one to let that cat out of the bag.

Life was good albeit boring most of the time. Ferreting out industrial espionage or hiring on as a security guard for wealthy clients was not as "sexy" as saving the lives of innocents, but it was a lot safer. If he never buried another friend or teammate, it was fine with him. There were enough ghosts following him around.

A gust of wind tickled the hairs on the back of Chase's neck as he reached for the bar door. It usually meant something was up. But why now? As he pulled it open, he decided to stay for one beer with Riot, then he was out of there. The flight home was early in the morning and made the perfect excuse to leave when things got uncomfortable. He wasn't sure how Riot would react. Did he blame him for his injuries? He'd recovered enough to be certified again for active duty, but Chase had been the one to lead them into that shit show.

The scent of beer and bar food reminded him of the last time he'd been there, and the memories sucked the air out of his chest and he stood still as they hit him like a slap in the face. Then the loud thump of music seeped into his mind and broke the spell. The music was new, not the old jukebox that had been in the corner of CC's Saloon for as long as he could remember.

Icy cold fingers of warning sent his Spidey-sense into hyper-drive. After he'd stopped being an operator, he'd expected it to disappear, but it hadn't and when it went off, there was a damn good reason. The only problem what reason could there be for it to go off now? The urge to get the fuck out of there was strong, but he'd never backed away from a challenge, and he wasn't going to start now. But it didn't mean he'd be happy about it either.

CC's Saloon was packed to capacity. That

was new too. It had been more of a neighborhood bar, filled with mostly Teams guys blowing off steam and women who wanted to "hook up" with them. As his eyes adjusted to the dim lighting, it became apparent just how much it had changed. The décor had been updated, they'd added at least triple the tables, and a stage in the center.

Scanning the room, he picked out Riot at a table close to the stage. Focused on making his way over to his table, he didn't notice Mick until she tapped him on the arm. Damn, so much for his Spidey-sense. Maybe his situational awareness needed some fine-tuning.

"Frost! Haven't seen you in ages. How the hell are you?"

"I'm great, thanks. It's good to see you, Mick. How have you been?" Chase pulled her into a quick hug then released her before she slugged him. She'd opened CC's Saloon over twenty years ago after her husband was killed in Desert Storm. There were rumors he'd been a SEAL, but no one knew for sure, or if they did, they weren't talking. CC's was practically a landmark although no one knew who CC was and

Mick wasn't sharing. "I thought I was in the wrong place. It's totally different."

"You know the drill, if you're not moving forward, you're falling behind. These new kids don't want jukebox music and greasy fries. I didn't even know what the hell kale was until some smart ass in a mini-skirt complained about the green shit in her salad. The new crop of frogmen isn't much better."

"Seriously? The Teams guys want salad?"

"Some of them. Maybe they get too used to eating grass during BUD/s. It's okay, we changed the menu, and it took care of the complaints and the lack of business."

"Everything is good?"

"Oh yeah, no one messes with me, they know better."

Chase chuckled. That was truth, no one dared mess with Mick or her sidekick, chef, and rumored boyfriend, Max. If anyone tried, he'd come out of the kitchen with a cleaver in his hand and God help the asshat who caused the trouble.

"You picked a good night to stop by, we're having one of our burlesque shows."

"Burlesque? Seriously? I guess things

changed more than I thought." She laughed again and patted him on the arm.

"For the better, trust me. Where are you going to sit? I'll bring you a beer on the house. You going to be hanging around for a while?"

"Afraid not. I'm heading back to Florida tomorrow."

"Well, damn. Hopefully you won't stay away so long next time."

Chase winked. "If I'd known you'd added strippers I'd have been back sooner."

Mick punched him and almost knocked him over. She had an arm on her. "Not strippers. Burlesque. Don't let those girls hear you call them strippers or there will be hell to pay."

"Yes, ma'am."

"Don't give me any of that ma'am bullshit either. You know better."

"Sorry," Chase said and attempted to look contrite but the twinkle in her eyes said he hadn't pulled it off.

"All right. Go sit somewhere and I'll be back with a beer. Same as always?"

"Do you remember?"

"Sure, I do. What do you take me for? You like whatever I've got on tap."

Same ole Mick. The decorations might be different, but she'd never change. Maybe it wasn't so bad being back after all. He worked his way through the maze of tables and throng of people until he made it to Riot's table. Chase made sure he approached him head on although the way he had his chair positioned it would have been hard to do it any other way. Everyone knew you didn't sneak up on a frogman and live to tell about it. Another thing that never changed.

"Riot."

"Frost. I was starting to think you were going to stand me up."

"The case took a little longer to wrap up then I expected, then Mick waylaid when I walked in. Holy shit this place has changed. At least she hasn't."

"Damn straight I haven't changed," Mick said as she put the frosty mug of amber liquid on the table. "Need a refill, Riot?"

"I'm good, thanks."

"Okay, enjoy the show. It's starting in about five minutes."

"Thanks, Mick." Watching her maneuver her way through the maze of tables was a thing of beauty. She wasn't a small woman, and the place was packed but she navigated through without hitting a thing. It wasn't the first time he wondered about her background.

"How long are you staying?"

"My flight leaves first thing in the morning."

"Damn, Boss. You didn't leave much time for socializing."

"To tell you the truth, I wasn't sure you'd want to see me. And I'm not your 'boss' anymore."

"It doesn't feel right to call you anything else. Old habits die hard."

"Ain't that the truth. How're you doing?"

"Better. It took awhile to get cleared for duty. I thought for sure I was going to lose my operator status."

The tension eased in Chase's shoulders as Riot talked about the last three years. It was good to see his friend back to his old self. It had been touch and go for weeks after the mission. Followed by months of rehab. It had been a miracle that he'd pulled through let alone be cleared for duty.

"You deserved it, I've never seen anyone work harder. When it first happened, I was happy you survived. I never thought you'd ever walk again."

"You always worried. A regular mother hen," Riot said with a grin. Shadows flitted across his eyes, but he blinked them away. "You know none of it was your fault, right? No one could have foreseen that shit." Chase wanted to agree but he couldn't. He was in charge, everything about the mission was his responsibility.

"Seriously, Boss, what do you go by? Frost? Chase? Stubborn asshole?"

"It's good to see you didn't lose your sense of humor. Chase works. Stubborn asshole fits you better."

"Fine, but you can't take responsibility for bad intel. You did everything you could to protect us. I hope you're not still carrying that shit around."

"I'm not. Working with Dr. Murdock helped a lot and being away from here helped with the rest."

"And now you're back and so are the memories?"

Chase swiveled his head to meet Riot's eyes. How did he know? Was his poker face letting him down? "Maybe."

"Before you flip out, I know because it still haunts me too. PTSD is a bitch. All we can do is keep a tight rein on it and move on. I'm not going to let it ruin my life."

"I'm proud of you."

"You and me both. But it's all good." Riot flashed one of his toothy grins, his bright white teeth glowing in the dim lights of the bar.

"Enough of this mushy stuff. How long has this been going on?" Chase gestured toward the stage.

"About six months. I got back from a mission and came in with the Team and it was all different. For the better, I'd say. I can bring a date here now."

"Dating? You mean there's a woman out there who will go out with you more than once."

"Fuck you. I…" Whatever he was going to say next was cut off when Mick's voice came over the sound system.

"CC's Saloon is happy to welcome back the Kitty Kats Burlesque troupe. Remember the rules, no touching. If you break them, Max will break you."

The bar had filled up while he and Riot were talking. Mick hadn't lied, he'd never seen it this crowded. Who knew burlesque was so popular. Hell, he wasn't sure what it entailed. When he'd called them strippers, it's because that's what he thought they did.

Riot leaned across the table. "Wait till you see these women. They're great."

Chase nodded rather than yell over the music. Leaning back in his chair, he turned his focus to the stage. The pre-show soundtrack faded, and the lights dimmed. A single spotlight focused on center stage as the doleful sound of *Royals* by Lorde echoed throughout the hushed room as the first dancer glided onto the stage.

There was something familiar about the way she moved as she shook and shimmied in black sequins and lace. It reminded him of the Flamenco dancers he'd seen in Spain. Every movement in sync with the music, every sway of her hips, every turn of her body like the music had been written for her. Seductive. Alluring. Spellbinding. Every face was focused on the stage and hypnotized by her every move.

A domino mask covered most of her face, but her ruby red lips were parted in invitation. He reached for his beer, parched from breathing through his mouth as he followed the sway of her hips and her gloved hands as they traveled over her body and released the layers of her costume. As the fabric slid to the floor, he swallowed a moan. It wasn't stripping, Mick was right. There was nothing crass about her performance. It was a seduction of every person in the room.

The masked woman owned the stage and the audience. It was mesmerizing to watch as she gyrated to the beat of the music. It was one hell of a performance.

He didn't know how many layers she removed, but when she slid the corset from her body, the silence broke. Cheering overpowered her music, but she didn't miss a beat. With another twirl her lace and sequined skirt slid down her legs and she kicked it to the side of the stage.

She. Was. Magnificent. Her voluptuous breasts were barely contained in her black sequined bra and the matching boy shorts encased her hips like they'd been painted on. Every curve accentuated, and with every shimmy, his mouth watered for a taste. He'd never experienced anything like it. Or not in a long time. There'd only been one other woman who'd affected him that way.

Chase wasn't sure how much more he could sit through, he'd already had to adjust a few times and he was in danger of popping his zipper. It had been ages since he'd felt this kind of arousal. After he'd left Faith, there hadn't been another woman to pique his interest. As the mysterious dancer melted onto the chaise that had appeared on the stage, all thought slid from his mind. Lifting her left leg high in the air, her glove-encased hands slipped from her ankle to her thigh.

His breath caught in his throat as she repeated her movements with the other leg and then she swung them onto the cushions and leaned back until her upper body hung over the edge. Upside down, she faced the audience. As her tongue moistened her ruby red lips, the spotlight faded to black as the music stopped. He'd bet good money that there wasn't a man in the room who didn't groan.

After a second or two of absolute silence the crowd erupted in applause. At least half of the men were on their feet, and without realizing it, Chase was too. She hadn't revealed any more than anyone at the beach, yet, it was so erotic, he'd swear she'd touched him.

"Holy crap. That was amazing."

Riot grinned. "She always is."

"What's her name? I know they announced it but for the life of me I can't remember."

CHAPTER 2

"Riven Heart," Mick answered from his side. Twice now she'd snuck up on him. It was sloppy. Good thing his life didn't depend on it.

"That was incredible."

"I knew you'd love it. We've been doing these shows with the Kitty Kats for about six months. The last few weeks I've had to turn people away. The Fire Marshall threatened to shut me down," Mick answered with a grin. "It's a first for ole CC's Saloon. These girls have put us on the map in Coronado."

"You've earned it."

"That's for damn sure, and because of it, I

don't want to see anything happen to these women."

Riot and Chase exchanged glances. "What do you mean? Did something happen? Does Max need help?"

"No, nothing like that. This is different. Do you have a few minutes to come to my office? I want to show you something."

"Of course."

"I'm coming too," Riot said as he pushed back from the table. Mick nodded in agreement and they followed her to the office behind the kitchen. The whole time, Chase ran scenarios in his head trying to figure out what was going on. It's what he did best, put together puzzles, and he hadn't come across one he couldn't solve.

Mick unlocked the office door and led them over to a box. It was wrapped in brown paper sitting in the center of her desk. It looked innocuous enough. No outward signs of a threat, but in this world of bombs in mailboxes it didn't hurt to take precautions. Chase exchanged a look with Riot and they waited for her to explain.

"Like I told you earlier, we've been doing these burlesque nights for about six months. It started as a favor for Riven Heart. She pitched the idea to me. Max and I talked about it and decided to give it a shot. It's just a side gig for her. Her real job is helping you guys. How could I turn her down? Besides, I was looking to change things up, there's lots of competition in Coronado now. All these yuppie bars. What kind of shit is that?"

Chase nodded as he listened to her round-about explanation. Mick could be chatty when she wanted to, but it didn't happen often. He could count on one hand the number of times he'd heard her string more than ten words together.

"Anyway, the girls got notes, flowers, all kinds of little gifts. It was innocent enough at first. But at some point, over the last few months it changed. The focus was on Riven, and some messages were pretty creepy."

"What do you mean creepy?" Riot asked before Chase had a chance.

Mick looked uncomfortable, the dancer had shared her worries in confidence and Mick wouldn't want to break that. For her to be talking to them it had to be serious.

"She's been getting stuff at work and her

house too. She didn't tell me at first, hell she didn't tell her friends either. But she's scared. The notes have gotten threatening."

"Has she called the police?" It's what he would have suggested. He had no jurisdiction in California or anywhere else. A private detective's license meant nothing to law enforcement.

"Yes, she did, but only after Max talked her into it. But they couldn't help. No real threats were made, and she hadn't been touched."

"Right, that makes sense. Doesn't help her though. So, what can we do?"

"This box came for her tonight. After she told us what was going on, we said we'd open them first. You need to see this."

They approached the box. He hadn't realized it was open. Grabbing a pen off Mick's desk, he pushed open the cardboard flaps. Someone filled it with paper hearts and what looked like a dead bird. But not one you'd find outside, this was bright yellow and green with pink cheek markings.

"That's a love bird," Riot said with a low whistle.

"I didn't realize you knew birds?" Chase

answered as he reached in with the pen to move the contents around, looking for anything else.

"Yeah, one of my neighbors has a pair. They're usually in pairs."

"Not this time," Chase said with a grim expression. "Was there a note?"

"Yes, it's over here."

Chase unfolded it with the pen. The note was short.

Beloved,

I hope you enjoy my gift. It's as beautiful as you are. I can't wait to have you all to myself.

He'd never seen Mick on the verge of losing it in all the time he'd known her. If it had been anyone else, he would have hugged her, but he valued his life. Luckily, Max walked in as if on cue and engulfed her in a huge bear hug.

The last thing Faith wanted was to be among the people in the audience. When Mick told her she'd gotten another box and what it contained, she'd freaked out. He had to be there, the stalker, and he could be anyone. Had to be one of them. He wanted her to know he was watching. As she made her way to the office with Max, she whispered her mantra under her breath. The repetition calmed her. He wouldn't do anything in public. There were way too many people in CC's.

How had he figured out who she was? Only a few people knew Riven Heart the burlesque dancer was Faith Murdock the psychologist. She'd been careful to keep her identity hidden while she performed. The last thing she needed was her patients or colleagues to find out. Dancing was her release from that world, her place to let go of everything she internalized. And there was plenty. Her patients were mostly SEALs, and they'd been through hell and back before they'd agree to come in for treatment.

The stalker situation had been escalating over the last four months. At first, she'd found notes on her windshield when she'd leave work. It creeped her out, but they weren't threatening. Then they'd morphed into phone calls and packages. She didn't tell anyone about the phone calls, but since some boxes were left at the club, she'd had no choice but to tell Mick about the others. Mick and Max had been her saviors once they'd finished ripping her a new one for not telling them sooner. There was only a small group of people she trusted, and she could count them on less than one hand. But she was a professional. She should have been able to handle this, shouldn't she?

It was unreal. She didn't understand what she'd done to warrant his attention. When the notes first started, she chalked it up to normal fan behavior. All three of them received notes, gifts and even a view requests for dates. It was fun in the beginning. Then it changed, at least for her. Her fan/stalker got insistent that she answer him, and when she didn't respond, he sent more notes, more packages. The letters got long and rambling. Her life became a horror movie. All she needed was a man in a white mask to show up. For the record, she hated horror movies.

She continued to ignore him, but instead of stopping it escalated. The hang-ups happened at all hours of the day and night. Then the dead flowers on her front porch. Somehow, he'd figure out where she lived, and it scared the hell out of her. She'd have been all over her patients for ignoring something like this. It was wearing on her, she couldn't eat or sleep. Her nerves were shot.

Tonight's package terrified her. The dead flowers were bad enough, but now he'd killed a bird because of her. Her heart hurt for the small life he'd snuffed out. What kind of person would do that? She'd racked her brain going over everyone in her life, but none of them presented with any kind of sociopathic or psychopathic tendencies.

After the one mistake three years ago, she made sure to never get too close to her patients, in fact, she did everything she could to keep them at arm's length. It's the main reason she'd gotten involved with burlesque. After losing Frost, she needed to work through her problems. Seeing an ad for dance classes, she'd signed up. That was where she met Syn LaRue and Honey Potter. After a year of classes, they started their own troupe and the Kitty Kats were born.

Syn was performing when Max came to escort her to Mick's office. Just seeing the six-foot-five inch tall, walking wall on the other side of her dressing room door helped her relax.

"Mick is waiting for us in the office. She wants you to talk to someone. We're worried about you."

What could she say? The dead bird horrified her. It was way too real now. What would be next? Would he hurt Syn or Honey? Or one of her patients? Looking at the faces, she wondered who he was. The hairs on the back of her neck stood up as it felt like a million eyes were on her.

"Who does she want me to talk to?"

"I don't think you know him. But she's known him for a long time and respects him."

Mick was an excellent judge of character, so there was no reason to doubt her assessment of the mystery man. Maybe he'd be able to help since the police couldn't.

Max kept her distracted as he led her through the crowd, without her mask and costume she looked like any other bar patron. It wouldn't matter, the stalker knew who she was so if he was there, she couldn't hide.

Max opened the office door and she came face-to-face with the man Mick wanted her to meet. Maybe she wasn't seeing clearly? Blinking changed nothing. The man who'd haunted her dreams since the day they'd met was standing in front of Mick's desk and examining the box. What on God's green earth was Frost doing there?

"Frost?" Faith said, her voice barely above a whisper.

His head turned toward her, and his eyebrows lifted. It was obvious he was as surprised as her. Mick hadn't told him her identity. Not that it mattered now. The Kitty Kat was out of the bag.

"Faith? Wait, that was you on stage?"

Her shoulders tightened and her back stiffened as she prepared for a fight. Meeting his eyes, she braced for whatever was coming next. After the stress of the last few months, she didn't need to hear his judgmental thoughts about her dancing or anything else. "Yeah. You have a problem with that?"

"Easy. You could cut the tension in here with a knife. Let's take it down a few notches. We're all friends," Riot interrupted Faith before she said anything else. She hadn't noticed him when she'd followed Max into the office. Big surprise, her focus had been on

Frost. After all this time, he still took her breath away.

"No, of course there's no problem. You took me by surprise. And for the record, you were freaking amazing," Chase said, admiration visible in his eyes.

Her hackles dropped back to where they belonged, and she tried to smile. Last she'd heard he was running a business in Florida. So, what was he doing standing in Mick's office? *Damn it, Faith, none of it matters, he's off limits.* "Thank you. Seeing you surprised me too. You're the last person I expected. You look good. Better. Looks like you've been taking care of yourself."

"Yeah." Faith felt the questions in everyone's mind. Mick didn't realize they'd known each other, or that he'd been her patient until they couldn't resist the attraction. She had a responsibility as his doctor and she'd pushed him away. It was the right thing to do, but her heart never recovered.

"I guess Coronado is a smaller place than I thought," Mick said with a twinkle in her eye.

"Looks like it," Max replied. Riot was still standing next to Frost watching their reactions.

It wouldn't take him long to figure things out. She hadn't treated him, but she knew of him. He'd been a member of Frost's SEAL Team and had been injured at the same time.

"It was a long time ago. I go by Chase now."

Faith nodded. It made sense, he retired so there was no reason for him to continue to use his nickname. Knowing what he'd gone through, he'd try to distance himself from it as much as possible. The years had been good to him, and he looked even better than the last time she'd seen him. But was he whole on the inside?

"Why are we all here?" Faith's head was spinning. Seeing Frost… Chase was enough to push her over the edge her nerves were so fried.

"I asked Chase if he could help. He's good at figuring stuff out."

Faith knew it all too well.

"You need help, girlie. We're worried about you. This guy is dangerous."

"I agree with Mick. He is dangerous, and from the look on your face, I bet there's a lot you've been keeping to yourself. Isn't there?"

Faith hated when he did that. He looked into her eyes and saw into her soul. "Maybe."

"You've been holding back on us?" Max asked with a disapproving look. "What about the girls? Have you told Syn and Honey? They could be in danger too."

"No, not all of it. I didn't want anyone to worry."

"Lord, save me from stubborn women," Max lamented and shook his head, which earned him an elbow in the side from Mick. You couldn't get much more stubborn than she was.

"Well until tonight it was just minor stuff. Notes, phone calls, dead flowers…"

"Wait? Phone calls? Dead flowers?" Mick's voice went up a few octaves. "Girl, are you trying to get hurt?"

"No." Faith wasn't sure if telling them would be a good idea or not but maybe it would ease some of Mick's worries. She opened her purse and pulled out the SIG Sauer. "I got my license and I've been going to the range a few times a week."

It was Riot's turn to shake his head. "And you're going to tell me you're prepared to kill someone with that gun? Because unless you can shoot to kill you have no business carrying that around. You'll only get hurt."

Chase nodded his head. She should have known they'd twist it around as something bad. She'd been so proud of herself for taking the steps to learn how to shoot so she could protect herself. But what Riot said sent a chill down her spine. Would she be able to shoot to kill if she had to?

CHAPTER 3

Holy shit. Faith. The woman who'd haunted his days and filled his dreams for the last three years. How did he miss it? On second thought, his body knew, it's his brain that was slow to join the party. Then again, the last person he'd expected to be a burlesque dancer was Dr. Faith Murdock. Not that she wasn't passionate. He could still feel her lips on his and the heat of her body pressed against him. Shit. It had been mind-blowing, perfect, and completely wrong. Once again, he'd fucked up. At least it hadn't killed anyone.

"Riot is right. More people are killed with their own guns because they freeze. It's not easy to shoot a person." She was trying to be brave and it made him love her even more, but it scared the ever-living fuck out of him too. Even his sub-conscious knew he loved her. Could this be a second chance for them? She wasn't his doctor anymore. Was there some kind of statute of limitations on that? What the hell was he doing, he wasn't fifteen with a hard-on every time the wind blew. She was in serious trouble. He needed to get his head in the game, it was not the time to be dreaming of hearts and flowers.

"I know that. That's why I've been going to the range."

"Target shooting is not even close to the same." Faith's chin jutted out. He recognized the look. She was getting ready for a fight. He didn't want to make her mad he wanted to keep her safe.

"He's right you know," Mick said. "I've seen it in action." They all turned toward her, and she shrugged her shoulders. Chase was seeing a whole other side to the bar owner. Funny how things pop out at the oddest times.

"Fine. But I feel safer with it."

"Let's table the gun discussion for now. We

need to know everything that's been going on, even the stuff you didn't tell Mick before."

Faith met his eyes with an assessing look, trying to analyze him, discover if he was as whole as he appeared. She'd met him when he was at his worst, but he wasn't that person anymore, mostly because of her.

"I'm in it for the duration if that's what you're wondering," he responded to her unasked question.

"What about your business in Florida?"

"I'm the boss I can do what I need to. And I'm staying here until we figure this out and I know you're safe." Max's grunt of approval from behind him almost made him smile but Faith was the one who needed to trust him. To let him into her world.

"As long as you're sure it won't be a problem. I can pay…"

"Stop. C'mon Faith. You know me better than that. Let's sit down and figure this out, okay?" He pulled out a chair and waited to see if she'd sit. After a deep breath, she walked over and sat down. Max brought in a couple more chairs and they all huddled around Mick's desk.

"I'm not sure where to start…"

"With the first contact you can remember."

After another deep breath, Faith seemed to center herself and the change was obvious. She'd assumed her psychologist persona. Calm and detached with a hint of fire in her eyes.

"It started about five months ago."

"What the hell, why…" Mick sputtered.

"Let her finish, I've already been down that road with her," Max interjected. "Go ahead, Faith."

"At first, it seemed innocent enough. Notes left on the dressing room door. A flower outside, or stuffed animals. You knew about all of that, so don't start. It was harmless. I wasn't sure it was the same person. Then one evening as I left work there was a note pasted to my windshield. That was the beginning. First it was just on base, then they started showing up at the VA hospital."

"He figured out who you were pretty quickly then? Was there contact before you started dancing here?"

"No, but this is the only place we dance."

"How the hell did he figure out who you are?" Riot asked as he ran his hand through his hair and met Chase's eyes.

"I don't know. But we'll figure it out. Hey, Mick. Think we can get a few drinks?"

"Good idea. Be right back." Max followed her out of the office and closed the door. Chase hoped it would make it easier for Faith. Obviously, she was close to them, but she was holding back. There was something she didn't want them to know.

"Faith, you need to tell us everything. It's the only way we can keep you safe." He covered her hands with his and squeezed them for encouragement. She'd been staring down at her clenched fingers. "Baby, look at me. I swear it will be okay."

His words had the affect he'd hoped, and her eyes met his.

"I can't believe this is happening, it's a nightmare."

"Yes, it is. But we're going to make it go away."

"You can't promise that."

"Yup, I sure can. I have a lot of assets I can call on. We'll figure it out."

"And you've got my help as long as I don't get spun up."

"Thank you, really. I almost feel like I can breathe again."

"Good..." Before Chase could ask his next question, Mick and Max returned with a round of beer, popcorn and a bottle of water that must be for Faith. He wasn't going to say anything, but he thought she could have used something a lot stronger.

"So, he knows where you work and left notes there too?"

"Yes, a couple of times a week at first, then it was every day. In the beginning, they were sweet, but when I didn't respond they changed, demanding I stop ignoring him. And no, before you ask, I don't have a clue who it is. I've racked my brain trying to figure it out. Every person I see I wonder if it's him."

"I wish you would have told us how bad it was," Mick said.

"I didn't think it was a big deal, not at first. I told you when it got worse and creeped me out. It was only on base or at the hospital then. But a couple of months ago, I found the first note at my house. It was waiting for me when I left for work in the morning."

"Your house? Riot repeated and shook his head.

"Yes. Then not long after that the calls started. It was always a blocked number, but you block your numbers and since mine is unlisted, I figured it was a patient. When I picked up, there was nothing, just silence then the call would disconnect. It started happening all hours of the night, so I changed my number. It worked for about a week, but then the calls started again."

"And you still didn't tell anyone?" Riot asked as he shook his head, disbelief painted on his face. Chase figured they were thinking the same thing. Except she was his woman even if she didn't realize it yet.

The looks on their faces told her how stupid she'd been to keep it to herself for so long. But she wasn't the damsel in distress type. She'd been on her own since she was eighteen and knew how to take care of herself. Until she'd met Syn and Honey and gotten closer to Mick, she didn't have anyone.

Making friends was never easy for her. Syn

and Honey were the closest she'd ever gotten to women her own age. Men were another story. The only one she'd ever fallen for was Chase, and he'd been forbidden fruit. As her patient a relationship with him would have broken all the rules. After growing up with her con artist father who spent more time in jail than out of it, Faith learned to follow the rules. They used to call her goody-two-shoes in college.

Being bounced between her father and foster care taught her it was better if she kept to herself. It was safer. Ironic that she chose a profession where she expected people to share their innermost feelings. It wasn't something she did well.

She didn't have a lot of life experience outside of dealing with her patients. Almost everything she knew about sex she'd learned from Honey and Syn's adventures. She was practically a virgin, if it grew back from lack of use, she would be. There were probably cob webs in there. She couldn't even remember what it felt like to have a man's hands on her. No, that was a lie. Memories of Chase's hands on her filled her dreams when she was able to sleep.

"Go on, Faith," Mick prompted.

"No, I didn't because it was still innocuous. Yes, he'd figured out where I lived. Looking back on it now, yes, I was stupid. I should have gone to the police then, but it wouldn't have made a difference. He hadn't done anything to hurt me." Stalling, she took a drink of water. "I've been so busy between work, volunteering at the VA, and the dancing. I tried to ignore it."

Chase looked like he was about to swallow his tongue. She knew him well, scratch that, she used to know him well. He'd never had a lot of tolerance for what he thought was stupidity. Not telling anyone what was going on was stupid and reckless. She worked with enough mentally ill people to know better.

"Last week, there was a bouquet of dead flowers sitting on my front stoop when I left for work. Later that day another note showed up on my car. It was the first time it really scared me. It said he was going to make it so I couldn't keep ignoring him."

"And that's when you called the police?" Chase asked.

"No, not yet. That's when I told Mick."

"And then Max made her call them," Mick interrupted. "We thought they could do more."

"At least the police have a record of it now. That's something," Chase mused and Max nodded. "Any more threats?"

"Sort of. They're vague, nothing specific. Mostly just long letters telling me I'll be sorry if I keep ignoring him. And how we're meant to be together."

"And then tonight, you got the bird…"

"Yes."

"He's definitely escalating," Riot said and Chase nodded. He was livid. Even the tips of his ears had turned pink. She'd only seen him like that once, after he'd punched a hole in her office wall during their first session. He really, really hadn't wanted to be there.

"Is that it?" Chase asked, but he looked toward Mick not her. She couldn't blame him for wondering if she was still holding back information.

"No, that's all of it. Isn't it enough?" It was a rhetorical question, she didn't expect an answer, and she didn't get one. Relief oozed through her. That she hadn't expected. It meant it had affected her more than she realized. *I guess that's why doctors make the worst patients.*

"We have to come up with a plan of action."

"I can go back to the police. I think it will be different now that he sent a dead animal."

"Yes, but I already told you. I'm here until I'm sure you're safe. Besides, my connections are much better than what the police have access to."

"He's right, Faith. You need to let us help you," Mick pleaded. The woman had done so much for her, given the Kitty Kats a place to perform, and been there whenever she needed her. It hit her hard, Mick was the closest person to a family that she had.

They were watching her, waiting for her to answer. If she was honest with herself, she had to admit it was a relief to share all of it and to know she didn't have to deal with it alone. The dead bird was the last straw and totally freaked her out. If he could do that, what was next?

"Okay, let's do this, but I want to try to keep Honey and Syn out of this. I don't want them getting hurt. So far, he's been focused on me. I'd prefer we keep it that way."

"How much do they know?" Chase asked, as

he typed into his phone. He wasn't wasting any time. She hoped he wasn't waking anyone up because of her.

"They know about the stuff that happened here—the notes, flowers, but they don't know about the stuff at home or work or the box tonight. I didn't want them freaked out too."

"Has the stalker contacted them at all?"

"I don't think so. They haven't mentioned anything weird. All the other notes we get are the usual types of things, phone numbers, email addresses, asking us for dates, that type of stuff."

"We'll try to keep them out of it as long as possible. But I really think you need to tell them. They have a right to know so they can take precautions. If we cut you off from him, he may try to get to you a different way. So, no promises."

She hadn't thought of that and a shiver of fear slid down her spine. The last thing she wanted was for anyone else to be hurt because of her. Shit, shit, shit.

"Okay."

"Did you happen to save at least some of what he's sent?"

"I have all of it except maybe the first few

notes he sent before I realized it was the same person. Everything is in a box at home."

"That was a really smart thing to do. Are you done for the night? Dancing, I mean?"

"Yes, why?"

"We need to get the box. I want to go through it."

"Can't it wait until tomorrow? I can meet you after work…"

His ears were pink again and there might have been smoke too. What did she say wrong now?

"No. We're not waiting. We're going to your house, we'll pick up the box and you can pack a few things. I'll get you a room at my hotel."

"Why would I do that? I've been home all along."

"That was before the dead bird, and before I found out about it. It's not safe for you to be there alone. You have two choices, the hotel or I'll stay with you at the house."

This was the Chase she remembered. A stubborn, pigheaded, frustrating man, but also right. It wouldn't have mattered either way once he'd made up his mind there was no way to budge him.

"There is another option," Mick interjected. "You can go get the box and Faith can come and stay with us." Max and Mick exchanged glances, and she shrugged. Everyone had wondered for years if they were together, now she knew. It was also a better option than being alone with Chase.

"I like that idea best." Chase wasn't thrilled, it was obvious from his expression, but there was no good reason or him to say no.

"Okay, but I want to go through the box and I might have questions."

"No problem, you can both come back to our place. We'll pick up where we left off here. Max has to close but I can get home."

"We'll be a little while. No hurries. We can always come back here and wait until you're ready."

They discussed her like she wasn't even there. It was infuriating. She crossed her arms and tried to get a word in unsuccessfully. Riot caught her eye and winked. She blew out her breath and shook her head. Then she realized Chase was staring at her waiting for something.

"What?"

"I asked if you were ready to go or do you have to get anything from the dressing room."

"Oh, yeah. I do. But it won't take long."

"I'll come with you." Of course, he would. She didn't know if that pissed her off that he thought she needed non-stop protection or thrilled that she got to be near him for a bit longer. As freaked out as she was by the stalker, being near Chase had brought back all the memories, all the longing. She'd forgotten how he made her heart pound and her pulse race and not just from frustration. Being around him was going to be hard, she'd put up so many walls last time and he'd broken them down, now there was no reason for the walls, except that he'd leave when she was safe.

CHAPTER 4

Chase needed to think fast. He wasn't about to let her out of his sight, and with her stubborn streak it wasn't going to be an easy feat. But she was in danger and he intended to be the one to keep her safe. He also needed to know if she still felt anything for him because his feelings hadn't changed.

The look she leveled at him didn't give much of an indication. She was nervous and upset, but was it all due to the stalker or was he affecting her too? He had to know. Not that it would change whether he helped her or not, but it would change the after. Their situation was different now, he was whole—mostly. And she wasn't his doctor. This time they could explore their feelings, not that he needed to, he'd been head-over-heels for her since the first time she told him to get over himself. But did she feel the same? And would he be an asshole for asking when she was dealing with all of this? He'd figure it out, but first he needed to get her alone.

Mick nudged Max in the side to get his attention. After his *oomph* from the unexpected elbow, his eyebrows rose, and he nodded. Chase admired their communication skills, not a word was said, but they clearly understood each other.

"Faith, are you okay with Chase going with you?"

After a moment's hesitation, she nodded. "Yes, but I'm fine going alone. I'll just run in, pack a bag, grab the box, and meet you at your house. I've been home alone all along and been okay. Why would that change now?"

"If there wasn't a dead bird sitting on Mick's desk, I'd say you're right, but nope. Either you wait until we close, or Chase comes with you. It's obvious there's history between you two, so whatever makes you comfortable is what we'll do." Chase was all for the second option, but like Max said it was up to her.

They waited as she bit down on her bottom lip. It was one of her tells and probably meant things weren't going to go his way. He'd give anything to know what she was thinking, and he willed her to say yes. There was more hinging on her answer than whether he could go back to her house, for him it was if she was going to push him away and deny them a second chance.

Over the years he'd analyzed every second of their last session. It had been wrong to step over the line, but he couldn't help himself. He'd given her the chance to stop him, to push him away, but it had been a moment of weakness for both of them. When their lips touched for that one and only kiss his world tipped sideways. Light shone where there had only been darkness. It changed him. Healed him more than all their sessions put together.

He hadn't seen her again after that—until now. She'd arranged for a new doctor and stopped answering his calls. Even with all of that, he didn't regret one second of the kiss.

"I'm going on the record as objecting to all of this. It's not necessary. But since I know you won't take no for an answer, I'll let Chase come with me and we'll meet you back at your house." It was obvious she wasn't thrilled with her choice, or maybe it was her options she didn't like when she started nibbling on her lower lip again. She'd always been independent. It shouldn't have been a surprise to any of them she wouldn't be happy about giving up control even if it was for her protection. She was too stubborn for her own good. Being stalked for almost six months without telling anyone until a few weeks ago was enough proof for anyone.

"Great. We'll see you in a while. Chase, behave yourself. Don't make me sorry I'm not coming with you," Max threatened as they got ready to leave.

"Give me a few minutes to go back to the dressing room and grab my bag."

"I'll come with you."

"I'm a big girl. I can handle this by myself."

"I know you can. But humor me. Okay?" She gave him an assessing look and nodded.

"See you in a little while. I'll make a pot of coffee. I have a feeling this is going to be a long night," Mick said as they left.

"I'll meet you at Mick's too," Riot added.

He finally had her alone. If being in the middle of a crowded bar could be considered alone. Once they got to the hallway where the dressing rooms were located they started to talk at the same time. Faith laughed, it was the first time since she'd walked through the door of Mick's office, and it was like a ray of sunshine.

"You go ahead," Chase said. He was curious what she'd say.

"Why do you really want to come with me? What's going on?" Not what he expected.

"There are a few reasons. The first being that you're in danger. The second is because I've been trying to figure out a way to see you again for years."

"Really? I figured once you left that you'd put all of this behind you." She gestured with her arms as they approached the dressing room.

"You figured wrong. I never forgot any of this, and especially not you." That stopped her in her tracks. He was glad he could still surprise her.

"I can understand not forgetting your SEAL life, but me? No reason for that. There wasn't anything between us."

"Wasn't there?" He needed to see if she still felt something, anything, and he watched her expression closely in the dimly lit hallway. But there it was. A blink, and then she sucked her bottom lip between her teeth. He still had a chance as long as he could keep her safe.

"It was one kiss." Yes, but what a kiss.

"It should have been more."

"No. It shouldn't/couldn't have been more. You were my patient."

"Only until you transferred me to Dr. Goldblatt. Then there was no reason to push me away."

"Yes, there was. You only thought you cared. It's common in doctor-patient interactions."

"You're wrong there, doctor. Or I wouldn't still dream about kissing you."

"What?" The look on her face was priceless. He couldn't resist the urge to lean down and kiss the surprised "O" of her lips.

The barest touch was all he accomplished before the dressing room door swung open to reveal two half-naked women.

"Well, what do we have here?" A tall blonde woman asked.

"Go back inside, Syn. Nothing, nothing at all. Don't even start," Faith answered before he could say a word. Rather than cause any more trouble, he flashed the women a smile and backed away from Faith. Her thoughts were unreadable now that she'd stepped away from him. He hoped he hadn't screwed the pooch by stealing the semi-kiss.

"I'll wait out here while you grab your things."

"Of course you will." Leaning against the wall, he listened to the chattering voices inside the dressing room but couldn't make out what they were saying. *Oh to be a fly on the wall in there right now.* From the way everyone reacted to his interest in her, his little doctor had kept their history a secret, but so had he. If he hadn't been so unsure of himself, of not trusting anything he felt, he wouldn't have let her push him away. Once he was finally whole again, he realized he'd made a huge mistake by leaving.

"Who is that guy?" Honey asked as soon as the dressing room door shut leaving Chase in the hallway.

"No one."

"Bull puckies, and you know it. You were

kissing him," Syn said. Honey nodded in agreement.

"No, he kissed me. I was just as surprised as you two."

"Sure you were. Spill it. We've known you for how long? We've never seen you let a guy touch you let alone kiss you."

Faith sighed. Tonight had been one mess after another. She hadn't thought about Chase in months, okay days, or a day, but still, for the most part, he was out of her brain. That was her story, and she was sticking to it. But now he was there, waiting to follow her home. Oh my God. How the heck was she going to get through however long she had to be around him, without falling into his arms, or worse, into his bed? It had been a close call three years ago but now the reasons for pushing him away didn't exist.

"Damn. She has it bad. Look at her."

"What? You're crazy, I'm just distracted."

"You do know him. You have to tell us. You know everything there is to know about us and all the deadbeats we've dated or screwed."

"Not only do I know, I know way too much. You guys don't know the meaning of TMI."

They giggled. There had been some fun nights sitting around after rehearsals drinking wine and talking about guys. Faith managed to avoid telling them about Chase although she did talk about a couple of college boyfriends. Usually Syn and Honey had so much to share they monopolized the conversations and that had been fine with her.

"Yeah, well we know you live vicariously through our escapades. And you'd be surprised what we haven't told you yet. Honey, remember that time…"

"Shhh, Syn, Faith has to tell us about the sex god in the hall."

"Yeah, spill it, girlfriend."

As she grabbed her bag and folded her costume, she thought about what she could tell them. There was no reason to hold back, he wasn't her patient, and she didn't have to share that part of it. That's when she caught her reflection in the mirror. Her cheeks were flushed a rosy pink. No wonder the girls were all over her.

"Tell us about him."

"His name is Frost, actually he goes by Chase now. I knew him awhile ago."

"Frost? Is he on one of the Teams?"

"Used to be. He's not anymore." She wiped the makeup off her face and brushed her hair. "I knew him when he was still a SEAL. We almost dated but it didn't work out. He left about three years ago, and I haven't seen or heard from him since." It wasn't really fair to Chase, but she didn't know what else to say without having to explain the whole mess. She liked Syn and Honey, but she wasn't ready to spill her guts about her history with him.

"And tonight he just showed up out of the blue? In time to see you perform? It's like a fairytale."

"No, no, no. It's not. Not even close. Remember the stalker?"

"Ugh. You don't think it's him, do you?" Faith only told them bits of information about the stalker but she was going to have to fill them in. Chase was right, by being around her they could be in danger. Who knew what he was capable of and she wasn't going to put her friends at risk.

"I thought about it at first, but he doesn't live in California. It would have been really hard for him to pull off all the stuff that's been going on. The coincidence made me wonder at first."

"Did you ask him?" Honey said.

"No. I didn't think about it. I was the one being grilled. I haven't been completely honest with you either. The stalking has been much worse than you know. He knows where I work and live and tonight he sent a dead bird to me. Thank God Max opened it first."

"Holy shit, girl. Why didn't you tell us?" Syn demanded. Faith winced, they were right, all of them, she shouldn't have kept so much to herself.

"I'm sorry. I didn't think you'd be in danger. He was only sending stuff to me."

"But we could have helped you, made sure you weren't alone going home, stuff like that," Honey said. "Don't you trust us? I thought we were friends."

"Yes, I trust you and of course we're friends. I just haven't had a lot of them and I guess I'm pretty shitty at being one."

"You sure are." They nodded in agreement.

"It won't happen again. I promise."

"Group hug." It was Honey's answer to everything, but if it made her feel better, Faith was all for it. She really hadn't been a very good friend.

There was a knock at the door as the hug was breaking up.

Chase spoke through the door. "You okay in there? It's been a while, and I'm just checking." Honey and Syn giggled when Faith rolled her eyes. It was going to be worse having him around than Mick and Max combined. SEALs. OMG.

"I'm fine. It hasn't been that long. Keep your pants on."

"Yes, ma'am. At least for now."

"Holy crap. He did not just say that."

"Yes, he did." Syn and Honey burst out laughing again. Faith didn't know whether to laugh or be angry. He was laying it on thick. But why was he? Had he been serious when he said he still thought about her?

"Faith, what are you going to do with him?" Honey asked.

"I have no flipping clue. But Mick wants me to stay at her place for a few days. So I'm going to grab some stuff and head over there."

"And your bodyguard?"

"He's not my bodyguard."

"Really? He sure is acting like he has the job. Maybe you should stay with him instead. I bet it would be a lot more fun."

"Damn, you two are horrible. I haven't seen him in forever. I don't even know him anymore."

Syn got a knowing look on her face. "C'mon, Faith. You are a psychologist. You know him as well as anyone. You're not fooling us. You are glowing when you should be scared shitless." Crap. It was enough she'd seen it, now they had too. She might not want to admit it, but her body sure remembered Chase.

"I'm not staying with a stranger. I'll be fine at Mick's. I'll text you tomorrow so we can set up a rehearsal. At least we have a few weeks off before our next show."

Honey pulled her into a tight hug. "Be careful, okay? You don't know what that lunatic will do next." Once she released her, Syn did the same thing. It really was nice to have friends.

"I'll be fine. Remember I have the watchdog outside," Faith said as she pulled open the door.

"Watchdog, huh? That works."

"Whatever." Then she turned to the girls and winked. They were right, she was too uptight about it. They were adults, there was nothing to stop them from getting together even if it was just for a few days. Nothing except the damage to her heart when he left again.

"Bye, Chase. Take care of our friend."

"I plan on it."

That's what she was afraid of.

CHAPTER 5

After the way he'd been around her troupe mates, it surprised her to see him become all business as soon as they went through the back door of CC's. Scanning the area, he took her elbow and led to her parked car.

"Give me your cell phone."

"Why?"

"I'm going to program in my number and put yours in mine. This way if you run into trouble on the way home or anytime, you'll be able to reach me."

"But aren't you following me home?"

"Yeah."

"Do you actually think something is going to happen while I'm driving?"

"Truthfully? I have no idea. The guy has been stalking you for six months. Then tonight he gives you a dead bird. It's obvious he's escalating, and if you were my client, I wouldn't let you out of my sight."

"But…"

"Exactly. I know how stubborn you are. So, if I suggested you leave your car here and we take mine, you'd give me a million reasons why it wouldn't work. Instead, you get my number."

She hated to admit he was right, and that he knew her so well. There was no way she'd leave her car there overnight. Just thinking about being without transportation freaked her out a little. It would mean she'd have to rely on others to help her. She didn't do the trust thing well.

"Okay."

"Okay? That's it?"

"Yeah. You're right, I wouldn't want to leave my car. So, okay." He looked surprised. Good, maybe he didn't know her as well as he thought. She wasn't all that stubborn. Just self-sufficient. She had no choice growing up, and it was just more comfortable for her.

"What's your address, I want to plug it into my GPS in case we get separated." She rattled it off as he typed it into his phone. She got into her car, and he climbed into the passenger seat. "You can drive me to my car so you're not waiting back here alone." She was going to object, but she wouldn't win, so why bother. Chase was like a force of nature. She wasn't a pushover but was nice to have someone take charge for a little while.

While she waited for Chase to get into his car and pull up behind her, she went over everything that had happened since she'd gotten to CC's earlier. The box was waiting for her, but there had been boxes before. Her stalker hadn't even been leaving things at CC's anymore they'd been at her house or at work. So why tonight? What triggered the change? She tried to remember what his last note said, but she couldn't remember the details. They'd been getting longer and rambling, hardly making sense. A sure sign he'd been coming apart. And the frequency meant he was escalating. She should have paid more attention.

The image of the dead lovebird, stiff and cold in the box, horrified her. She couldn't kill a bug and seeing anything dead tore her up. Who did she know that was so warped they'd send her something like that?

A tap on her window made her jump. She'd been so wrapped up in trying to figure out everything that she hadn't realized Chase had pulled up behind her. Pressing the power window button, it slid open.

"Are you okay?"

"Yeah, sorry. I was thinking."

"Are you sure you're all right? We can still leave your car here."

"I'm fine. I promise."

"Then lead on, my lady. I'll be right behind you."

"Try to keep up." Pulling out of the parking lot, she kept a slow pace so as not to lose him. It wasn't a long drive, only about fifteen minutes from CC's without traffic, and that time of night it was lighter than usual. She checked her rearview on and off to make sure he was still behind. The whole situation was surreal.

When they arrived at her house, she pulled into the driveway, and he parked at the curb. Before she had a chance to grab her bag from the back, he was already at her side.

"Thank you, but I can handle it."

"Yes, you can but I want to. You've had a rough evening, it's the least I can do." It was late and dark, only the streetlights and the lights above her garage and front door add illumination and it was too dim to get a read on his expression. Was he being sarcastic or serious? In the past, he'd often covered up his true feelings under the curtain of sarcasm and had done it well.

The porch light shined pale yellow over her front door, but she wasn't looking at it, instead she was fiddling with her keys.

"You should have they key out before you get out of the car," he said from behind her. Before she could answer, he grabbed her shoulder. His touch sent a bolt of electricity skidding along her already frayed nerve endings, and her breath hitched in her throat. *Holy honey bees.*

"What's wrong?" She glanced up at him, but he was staring at her door. "Oh my God. Is that…"

"Yeah, it is. Let's get you inside, and I'll take care of it."

The tingle of desire she'd felt at his touch dissipated like a puff of smoke, morphing into terror. Two squirrels had been nailed to her door in the shape of a heart, their blood leaving trails down the length of the door and onto the stoop. How sick did someone have to be to do that? And Chase wanted her to go inside? He must be out of his mind.

Her first instinct was to get away as quickly as possible. He must have sensed her hesitation because he turned her away from the door and with the tip of a finger changed her focus to him.

"I'm sorry you had to see that. But I'm sure as hell glad I was here, and you weren't alone. We're going to go inside. I need you to stay by the front door while I check the house. Okay, Faith?"

She started to object, but common sense stopped her cold. What if the stalker had gotten inside? Chase took her keys and unlocked the door. She tried to avoid the poor dead animals as she went inside, but it was like a train wreck or a car accident, and she couldn't pull her eyes away.

While she waited for him to make sure her house was safe, she thought about all the times she'd imagined him in her home. None of them had been to check for a lunatic who seemed to be growing more unhinged by the minute. It was weird that he'd escalated so quickly. There had to be something she was missing. Obviously, he'd interacted with her at some point during her day or he wouldn't know so much about her. People don't pick arbitrary individuals to stalk. She learned that in her first year of college.

"It's all clear. It'll be okay, baby, I promise. I won't let anything happen to you."

Not only had he checked every room and all the closets, but he'd also turned on every light in the house. It was lit up like a Christmas tree, but she still had the creepy crawlies and wanted to get out of there as fast as possible. At least, if he'd been hiding, Chase would have found him. "Thank you."

"It's what I'm here for. It's a nice place, it fits you. While you pack your stuff, I'll take care of your front door. Will you be okay?"

"I think so. What are you going to do with them?"

"Bury them in the yard. Unless that's a problem?"

"It's fine." Those poor little things had died on her account, it seemed fitting that her yard be their final resting place. Maybe she should look into getting a big, mean dog. The stalker would think twice then, wouldn't he?

"Don't forget the box of goodies."

"Huh?"

"The box of stuff from the stalker. If I'm done before you're ready, I want to take a look."

"Don't you want to wait until we get to Mick's?"

"I'll just read whatever I have time for while you're getting your stuff together. I'm not going to go through the whole box."

Chase found a hammer and shovel in her garage. The tools made it a lot easier to pry the carcasses off the door. The asshole had meant to make them hard to remove. Faith wouldn't have been able to do it without help. What kind of psycho would first kill and then nail them to her door? And in the shape of a heart. It didn't make sense. Why the sudden escalation? If this had been going on for six months, what changed? Was Faith still holding something back?

The horror on her face was like a kick in the gut. His one job was to protect her. It was what he did, but so far, he'd done a piss-poor job. He'd been in such a hurry to get her inside he never thought to check the perimeter before she got out of the car. He needed to keep his head in the game. Whoever was doing this needed to be caught. Now that he'd stepped up his game to murdering animals the next logical step would be the object of his obsession. There was no way he was going to let the psycho get his hands on Faith.

Once the squirrels were buried, and he'd washed the blood off the front door, he went to check on Faith. "It's just me. Everything's all cleaned up."

"Okay. I'll be out in a minute. I'm just about done. The box is on the dining room table." He'd seen it when he came in. Anticipating a shoebox sized box, he was surprised when it was the size of a case of printer paper. She hadn't been kidding about him leaving notes almost every day. It was lucky she'd kept them. Most people would have tossed them hoping to forget they existed. But now there was a chance he could figure out who the guy was and track him down before he did any more harm.

As he sifted through the box contents, he glanced up to look out the window in time to see a car drive by. It could have been random, but his gut told him otherwise. It was too slow, whoever was driving was checking out her house.

"Be right back," he yelled as he ran out the front door. If he couldn't catch the car, maybe he could at least get a license plate number.

The driver must have seen him because he hit the gas as soon as Chase reached the driveway. "Damn it." Not fast enough to get more than the first three letters of the California license plate, but he did get a good description of the asshole's car—a late model black mustang. The way it took off it had to be turbocharged. It was better than nothing and hopefully enough to be able to track it down.

Faith was waiting near the front door when he got back inside. "What happened? Are you okay?"

"I'm fine. But I think your stalker did a drive-by. Probably to see if you'd found his latest 'gift'."

"No way." The color drained out of her cheeks. It looked like she was about to pass out and he pulled her into his arms. She'd had a hell of a night on top of dealing with all of this alone for so long. There was nothing he could do about the past, but he'd do whatever it took to protect her now.

"Baby, it'll be okay, I promise. I won't let anything happen to you." He held her close hoping to reassure her.

"How can you say that? You don't live here. You can't keep me safe." Her voice hitched as she fought to hold back tears. Her pain tore him up and set off all his protective instincts.

"I'm not going anywhere."

"Don't be silly. You have a business to run." She pulled out of his arms. The color slowly flowed back into her cheeks. She'd recovered faster than he'd expected. She wasn't some wilting flower, but it didn't mean she didn't need protecting.

"It can run fine without me there. You're more important."

"How can you say that? All we shared was one kiss, it's not like we were in a committed relationship."

"Faith, this isn't the time or how I wanted to have this conversation. But I'm in love with you, I was in love with you then, and I never stopped loving you. If my head hadn't been so far up my ass that I couldn't see daylight I would have realized it before I let you disappear from my life."

"You're right, this isn't the right time. I can't deal with it right now. I need to get out of here." He should have kept his big mouth shut, it was too much too soon, especially after the shock she'd just had. What the hell was wrong with him? He was thirty-six years old, not some horny eighteen-year-old. Max was going to have his ass in a sling before too long.

"You're right, and I'm sorry. I lose all common sense when I'm around you. We'll talk about it later."

"Thank you."

"I'll grab the box and you... Holy crap. Are you moving out?"

She followed his gaze to her two large suitcases. "Umm, no. Maybe. I don't know. I'm not sure I'll ever feel comfortable living here after tonight."

He couldn't blame her. But it was such an about-face from earlier. He really was an asshole, laying his feelings on her. "I understand. Well, I'll take your bags. Can you carry the box?"

"Of course. But I can…" His look must have conveyed his point, and she didn't bother finishing her protest.

"We'll take your car."

"What about yours?"

"I'll get someone to drive me over to pick it up later or tomorrow. I don't think you should be alone or driving right now. And since we've already had the discussion about leaving your car behind, we'll do it this way." He grinned, and she gave him the hint of a smile in return. It was a start.

CHAPTER 6

The porch light was on, just like the ad for the motel chain. Max must have been watching for them because as soon as Chase pulled into their driveway, the front door opened. Faith had to admit it was almost like having a family to come home to.

"What took you so long? You're lucky I didn't show up, especially when you didn't answer your phone," Max said when he opened her car door. He didn't even look surprised that Chase was driving her car.

"Oh God, I'm so sorry. It was in my purse and I didn't hear it ring."

"That's what Mick said, and it's the only reason we didn't drive over there."

"There were a few complications. But I want to get Faith inside. Then we can discuss it," Chase said as he opened the trunk to get out her suitcases. Complications, they could call it that, but it would be months and months before she'd be able to close her eyes and not see the dead squirrels on her door.

"We stopped at the store on our way home, so we have snacks too." Snacks? Faith wasn't sure she could swallow water, let alone food. But the low rumble in her stomach reminded her she hadn't eaten since lunch, and that was way too many hours ago.

"You didn't have to do that."

"Of course, I did. Or I'd have been sleeping on the couch." He followed that with a wink and for a second Faith was envious of their relationship. Even though they worked hard to keep it mostly under wraps if you were around them enough you knew how much they cared about each other. Faith didn't know much about their background, except that Mick's husband was a SEAL who'd been killed during Desert Storm and after that she opened CC's. The story goes that Max served with her husband and she hired him when he retired. She had no doubt that they'd lay down their lives for each other in a heartbeat. Love like that didn't come around every day.

"C'mon, slowpoke," Chase teased as he came up behind her with the box of evidence. While she'd been daydreaming, Max and Riot had grabbed her suitcases, and she was holding them up.

"Everything okay?" Mick asked as they came through the door. Faith wasn't sure who the question was directed toward, but she answered anyway.

"Yes, no, not really."

"What happened?"

"Let's sit down, and we can talk about it," Chase interrupted.

"In the kitchen, so we can look at what's in that box," Max added. "I'll bring these downstairs. Be right up," he said referring to Faith's suitcases. Seeing her oversized bags in his hands made her wonder if she'd overreacted. Then she remembered her door and all the blood.

Mick poured coffee for the guys and gave her a bottle of water. After Riot dumped the contents onto the table it surprised her to see how much was there.

"He sent all of that?" Mick asked as she pulled out a chair to sit down.

"Yeah." Faith wanted to kick her own butt once she realized how often he'd contacted her. Maybe those innocent squirrels would still be alive if she'd done something. The bird too. She'd been responsible for their deaths when her whole focus was preserving life. She'd sure made a mess of things.

"Max, do you want coffee or something else?"

"Coffee, thanks." He looked as surprised as the others when he saw the sheer number of notes, envelopes and small packages she'd gathered, the only thing she hadn't saved were the bouquets of flowers.

After they were settled at the table, they pulled a few of the envelopes from the pile.

"You put dates on everything?" Chase looked impressed.

"Yeah. I don't know why I started doing it but once I started, I kept it up."

"It was brilliant, baby. It will make it easy to see the pattern of escalation."

The use of the endearment threw her for a moment, then she realized he'd been doing it since her house. When she met Chase's eyes, he shrugged. It wasn't a big deal unless she turned it into one. It would be so easy to give in and let him take care of her and handle everything. But what about when it was done, and he went back to Florida? She'd be stalker free but would her heart recover from losing Chase twice in one lifetime.

"At least I did something right."

"You do plenty right. You're just too stubborn for your own good."

"He sure knows you, huh?" Mick commented with a grin.

"I don't know what you're talking about," Faith said, and they laughed. It was good to be able to relax a little. Her shoulders were so tight she could have bounced a quarter off them.

"How about you tell us what happened at Faith's?" Riot asked. With his words her tension increased tenfold.

"The bastard killed a couple of squirrels and nailed them to her front door in the shape of a heart."

"What?" Mick looked as horrified as Faith felt.

Max whistled. "No wonder you packed so

much stuff. Two huge bags for a few days seemed excessive even for a woman."

Mick elbowed him in the side. "Not everyone packs like the military."

"I'm sorry. I'm not moving in, I promise. But I can't go back there, not right now. Maybe not ever. I don't know how I'll ever walk through that door again."

"Don't worry, you're welcome to stay here for as long as you want. Right, Max?"

"Thank you, I appreciate it more than you know."

"You are family, we told you that. When is it going to sink in?" Faith wished she knew. Family was a hard concept for her.

"That reminds me. When I came in from burial duty, I caught a look at her stalker. At least I think it was, he was driving too slowly for it to be anything else. I grabbed a partial, but he saw me and floored it before I could get the whole plate. I'll email my guys. Hopefully they'll be able to turn up something. Of course, there's the chance it's a stolen car, and we'll still be at square one," Chase said.

"True," Riot commented. "I can see if any of my team can help if you want?"

"Maybe, let's see what I can turn up first. I don't want to get anyone into trouble."

"Sure."

"Damn…".

"Don't worry, we'll get him. I promised, didn't I?" Chase said, and that's when she realized she'd said it out loud.

"I know. I was just hoping for a break."

The guys took turns reading the notes while Faith and Mick organized the pile into chronological order. It took a few hours to get through all of them. That's when Faith realized he didn't leave a note with her "present" at the house.

"That's weird. He left a note every time, even if it was with something else like the flowers, or the bird earlier. But we didn't find a note at the house."

"Maybe I missed it. Shit. I need to go back and see if I can find it."

"I'll go with you. We shouldn't be long," Riot said.

"I'm coming too," Max said as he stood up and stretched.

"Great, it'll give me a chance to pick up my rental."

"Do you want me to come too?"

"No, we're just looking for the note. And I want to look around too," Riot answered, and Chase nodded. She really didn't want to go, but she felt responsible.

"You've been through enough already tonight. Just try to relax, we'll be back soon," Chase added.

"We'll have girl time while they're gone. I think wine is called for, don't you?" Mick said.

They'd barely made it out of the driveway before Max started the interrogation. Chase had expected it. He and Mick had taken her under their wing and they weren't going to let anyone hurt their girl.

"What's going on between you and Faith?"

"My intentions are true. If that's what you're asking. Three years ago, we had the beginning of something. I blew it and let her get away."

"I need more than that. You can't just drop out of nowhere and make promises then waltz out like some prima donna."

"I know that. After my last mission, they

made me go to counseling, and she was my doc. She got me to talk to her, and the more I saw her, the more I realized how much she meant to me."

"You know that's common, right? Are you sure you're not building this up in your mind? And it's been three years? A little long to wait, no?"

"Believe me I know. It took me a while to figure my shit out. The new doctor she referred me to helped me work through a lot, but I couldn't get past losing the team. I still have nightmares about it. How could I come to her when I wasn't whole?"

"You were way fucked up back then. I can attest to that," Riot said from the driver's seat. He glanced at Max in the rearview.

Max nodded. "I get it, I really do. But I don't know how successful you'll be."

"I kissed her three years ago. It's what freaked her out and made her walk away. She wouldn't answer my calls or text messages. She told me that even if she wasn't my doctor, she had been and we couldn't be together."

"She was right. It would have caused her a lot of trouble. She could have lost her license."

"I know. And I was a wreck. She was the only sunlight in my life. But I couldn't hurt her, and I wasn't in any place to plead my case, so as soon as I could retire, I did. Then I went to Florida to lick my wounds."

"And now? You didn't come back for her, tonight. It was a coincidence, right?"

"Yes. But I feel like fate is giving me a second chance. I should have tried to contact her. But I'm telling you, until recently my head still wasn't straight. Working one of my cases straightened it out for me. Showed me what was important. There isn't a day that goes by that I don't think about her."

"This isn't exactly the best time for her right now."

"No shit. But when is the best time? If I can convince her I love her and will do everything in my power to protect her then maybe that's exactly what she needs."

"You might be right."

Chase had been so invested in proving his case to Max he hadn't realized they were already at Faith's house. It was still lit up inside. He hadn't thought about turning off the lights earlier, his only concern had been getting her out of there.

"So, are we good?" Chase held his breath while he waited for Max's answer. He was surprised how relieved he was when it came.

"Yeah, we're good. But you better not hurt her. That woman has been through more than enough."

"I promise, and if I screw this up, you can kick my ass and send me packing."

"Deal. And don't you think for a minute that I won't."

"No doubt. But it's a moot point." He had no intention of Max or anyone else kicking his butt over Faith, but he was comforted to know he had her six. If he couldn't convince her to give him a chance, at least she'd be protected.

The neighborhood was quiet, but it was almost three a.m. There weren't any cars around, and the men started their search for any sign of a note. Even though the outside lights were on, they'd brought flashlights. Mick gave them some latex gloves, so they couldn't contaminate any evidence in case if they found anything.

They checked all around the front of the house and were about to give up when Riot spotted something sticking out from under the edge of one of the planter boxes. Sure enough, it was the missing note. It was odd he hadn't left it out in the open like the others. Maybe he'd been spooked before he had a chance to leave it where she could find it.

It was plain white paper and folded in half. There was nothing that stood out. And most likely it could have been printed on any laser printer.

Beloved,

I thought we had something special and then I see you with those asshole SEALs. They think they're so special, but you'll see soon enough that I'm the only one who can take care of you.

I hope you like your present. I went through so much trouble to make it pretty. Soon you'll be mine forever, here and ever after.

"This guy is a piece of work. And it confirms that he stayed to watch the show. He's obsessed, and it was an opportunity to see more of her."

"He has some serious issues."

"Forever here and ever after. I don't like the sound of that."

"I'm just glad Mick brought us in on this," Riot said as they headed toward their vehicles.

"Riot, are you coming back to the house?"

"I think I'll head back to my apartment. I need to check on my woman. I'll catch up with Chase tomorrow."

"Okay."

"You're coming back, right?" Max asked Chase.

"Yeah, if you don't mind. I know it's late, but I'd like to talk to Faith if she's still awake."

"No problem. I don't think any of us will get much sleep tonight. If we're lucky, we'll hear from your team sooner than later."

As Chase approached his rental car, he had his own surprise—four flat tires. The guy must have come back after he took Faith to Mick's house. He'd have to call for a tow but it could wait until tomorrow. "Hey, Riot. Hold up. We're going to need you to drop us back at Mick's house. My car isn't going anywhere."

Seeing the slashed tires, Riot said, "Damn. I guess you have a fan too."

"Oh yeah. But I can take whatever he wants to dish out as long as he leaves Faith alone." Before he got into Riot's car, he scanned the area but didn't see or hear anything. Something was off, but other than the slashed tires everything looked fine.

CHAPTER 7

After the guys left for Faith's house, Mick grabbed a bottle of wine and two glasses, and they went to wait in the living room. It was more comfortable than sitting at the table, and it kept Faith from staring at the piles of notes.

"Quite a day, huh?"

"Oh yeah. Not exactly how I pictured tonight at all."

"I'm sure. How are you holding up?"

"I'm not going to lie, the bird was bad, but the squirrels are going to give me nightmares for a long time. Nailing them to the door in the shape of a heart. How sick does he have to be?"

Faith took a swallow of wine and almost choked when it burned the back of her throat.

"Do you want some water?"

"No, I just need to sip and not gulp it." She tried to smile but figured she hadn't pulled it off when Mick's brow wrinkled.

"You know it's not Chase right? I saw that look when you recognized him. It surprised me that you two knew each other. Weird coincidence, huh?"

"That's for sure. I don't usually believe in them, but it really does look like it was just that."

"And how do you feel about it? About him? It's been a long time."

"Hey, who's the doctor here?"

"Sorry. But I'm curious. I knew him back when he was on the Teams and he was always a good guy. They'd come into the bar whenever they were in town. I know he took it hard when he lost them."

"He did. For a while, I wasn't sure I'd be able to bring him back from it. But he seems to be in a good place now."

"Yeah, he does. And very into you."

Faith thought about their conversation at

her house earlier. It had taken her by surprise, but maybe it shouldn't have. He'd always been intense and told her exactly how it was. He believed what he told her that much was crystal clear. Her body had responded to him like they'd never been apart. That one kiss had branded her, and his touch renewed all those old feelings.

"Faith?"

"Sorry. I was thinking about something Chase said to me earlier."

"Want to share?"

"He told me he's in love with me."

"Wow. I didn't see that coming."

"Neither did I. If I can believe him, he's never forgotten me and just didn't know what to do about it."

"For three years? Men can be such idiots."

"Right? It's my job, and I still don't understand how they think sometimes."

Mick smiled. "Probably not a good idea to go around admitting that. You might be out of work."

Faith giggled. "You're right. I can see it now. It'd be news at eleven, Naval psychologist admits to not understanding half her patients."

They'd almost finished the bottle of wine by the time the guys returned, and they had a case of the giggles. Maybe wine on an empty stomach hadn't been the best idea, but it was too late now.

"You both look a little too happy."

"Not us. We're just right," Faith answered and Mick giggled too. Max and Chase exchanged glances, and she figured they were thinking, 'women.' Which made her giggle harder considering the conversation she and Mick just had about men.

Chase sat on the sofa next to Faith, but Max went into the kitchen. When he returned, he had two beers and handed one to Chase.

"Thanks."

"Welcome."

"Did you find anything," Mick asked, after Max sat next to her.

"Yeah, we did. It was tucked under one of the planter boxes."

"I guess that's good, right?"

"I don't know about good, but it means he's keeping to type."

"What did it say," Faith asked, not sure she really wanted to know.

"We can talk about it tomorrow. You're relaxed, it's late. Probably a better idea to just drop it for tonight." It sounded like a good idea to Faith. She'd like to drop everything. Everything except Chase, she'd like to jump him.

"Damn."

"What's wrong?" Chase asked. She'd done it again. Spoke her inner thoughts out loud. No food and too much wine were a bad combination.

"Nothing. I didn't mean to say that out loud. I guess I was hoping he'd skipped the note this time." He nodded at her explanation, but she didn't think he believed it. Good, she wouldn't have either if she were him. She almost giggled thinking about it. Oh dear, she was in serious trouble. "What kind of wine was that? I think I'm a little tipsy."

Mick burst out laughing. "Yeah, I'd say so. Your cheeks are bright pink, and you keep giggling." Damn and double damn. She knew better. If she wasn't careful, she'd be saying all kinds of things she'd be sorry for in the morning.

"Is it okay if I crash here tonight? I'd rather not call a taxi this late," Chase asked.

"I thought you were picking up your rental car when you went back to my house."

"I was, but it had a few issues. I'll need to call for a tow tomorrow."

"What aren't you telling us?" Mick asked as she looked back and forth between Max and Chase.

"It's not a big deal," Max answered.

"They don't want to tell us. The ass clown stalker of mine must have done something." She tried hard not to giggle while she was talking but it wasn't working, then she hiccuped. She fell over into Chases's side and kept laughing.

"I think it's bedtime for the doc. Show me where to take her, and I'll get her tucked in."

"I can do it myself," Faith said and then hiccuped again.

Mick shrugged. "She only had two glasses of wine. She's not usually such a lightweight. Faith, did you eat today?"

"Ummm, yeah, maybe. I think so."

"Well that was definitive," Chase said wryly.

"Mick, do you have any crackers? I think she might need a few, so she doesn't end up getting sick. It's probably just a stress overload. I've seen it before."

"So have I. Chase is right. And yeah, you're welcome to stay the night. We have a lot to discuss in the morning, it'll be easier if you're already here."

"Thanks. Now about those crackers?"

Armed with crackers and a couple of bottles of water, Chase half carried, half dragged Faith down the stairs to the guest room. It had a bed, a dresser and a couple of chairs and a small table.

"How are you feeling?"

"Fine."

"Are you sure? Do you want some water?"

"Geesh, Chase. I just had two glasses of wine, I wasn't out tying one on."

The thought of her in a bar getting drunk made him laugh, and she started giggling again. It was adorable. He'd never seen her like this before.

"I never said you were."

"Good." *Hiccup.*

He put the water bottles and crackers on the table so she wouldn't see him smile and think he was laughing at her. He was but not in the way she'd think.

"I think I'll take that water now." She'd climbed onto the bed and was stretched out on top of the covers.

He loosened the cap so it wouldn't be hard for her to open and sat next to her. "Do you want me to cover you up?

"Okay." He dragged the quilt out from under her legs and pulled it up around her, but resisted the urge to tuck her in. It would have made it hard for her to hold the water bottle.

There was so much he wanted to say, but he kept his mouth shut. He should go upstairs, stretch out on the sofa, and try to get some shut-eye. It was the right thing to do. The longer he stayed with her, the greater the chance he'd do something he shouldn't.

"Do you have everything you need, baby?" The endearment slipped out, but he wasn't sorry.

"Yeah." *Hiccup.*

"I think you need some more water."

Giggling again, she tried to take a drink and ended up spilling half of it down her chin. She was too cute for words. He was dying to kiss her moist lips and use his tongue to catch the drop of water teetering on her lower lip. When her tongue slipped out from between her lips and licked it, he groaned.

"Are you okay, Frost, I mean Chase." Another giggle.

"Yeah, I'm fine. I'll head upstairs and let you get some sleep."

"No. Please don't go. Can you lie down with me?"

"Are you sure? Earlier you didn't even want me around."

"I changed my mind, it's a woman's prerogative isn't it?" *Hiccup, giggle.*

"Okay." He wasn't sure it was a good idea, but if she wanted him to stay close wild horses couldn't drag him away. He'd waited so long to be this close to her. There was no harm in that, right?

After kicking off his shoes, he stretched out on the bed, and she slid closer. Turning onto her side, she put her head on his chest, and he wrapped his arm around her until she was tucked up against his side. "Are you comfortable?"

"Yes, thank you.

"Good." She was quiet, and he wondered if she'd fallen asleep. Then she hiccuped, followed by another giggle. She might have been thirty-something, but she could have been a first time drunk teenager. He hoped she didn't wake up with a hangover.

"Why are you here?"

"You asked me to stay."

"No, silly. Why are you in Coronado?"

"I had a job in San Diego. After I finished, I gave Riot a call to see if he wanted to meet before I went back to Florida. He suggested we meet at CC's."

"Interesting coincidence."

"Yeah, you could say that."

Hiccup.

"Do you really love me?"

"Yes, baby, I do. I'm sorry I dumped that on you. How about we forget about it until after we catch your stalker?"

"Yeah."

"Close your eyes and get some rest. We'll talk in the morning."

"Okay. Umm, Chase?"

"Yes, baby."

"Don't leave."

"I won't." She cuddled closer, and her breathing slowed and evened out. He turned off the lamp and settled in for the night. Her hiccups finally stopped and as he listened to her breathe, he wondered if she'd only meant for the night, or forever.

"No, please don't. Don't touch me."

Startled awake by her cries, Chase didn't remember falling asleep. "Baby. Faith. Shhh, it's just a nightmare."

"No, no. Get away from me."

Gently shaking her, hoping to pull her out of whatever terrible dream had her in its grip. When that didn't work, he rubbed his hand along her cheek and felt her tears. Damn. She was crying in her sleep. But she didn't wake up, just continued to struggle in his arms.

He reached for the light and flipped it on then sat up and pulled her onto his lap. Finally, she opened her eyes and blinked as her eyes adjusted to the light.

"What's going on?"

"You had a nightmare. Don't you remember?" He wasn't sure she was fully awake, but then awareness flashed in her emerald eyes still shiny with tears.

"Oh my God. He was chasing me. I couldn't see his face, but he kept repeating that I was his and no one could stop him." She shuddered and wrapped her in the quilt.

"It was just a dream, baby. He's not here, and I'm not going to let him get to you. Neither will Riot or Max. You're safe." He prayed he was right.

"I'm sorry I woke you."

"Don't worry about that. I'm glad I was here. It scared me when I couldn't wake you. I don't know if it was the wine or you're just a sound sleeper."

Her hint of a smile warmed his heart. "A bit of both, probably. I'm not used to drinking on an empty stomach."

"Do you want some crackers?"

"Nah, I'm good. I feel okay." As if to verify it, she yawned. "Can we shut the light off and go back to sleep?"

"Sure. Do you still want me to stay?"

"Yes, as long as you don't mind. It can't be very comfortable. But having you here makes me feel safer." He wasn't sure whether she realized how much she revealed with that one sentence but he'd take great pleasure reminding her when the time was right.

This time he didn't fall asleep as quickly. He wondered if her dream meant that somehow she recognized her stalker on a subconscious level. He didn't like the idea of pushing her to try to remember, but it might be their best chance of catching him.

CHAPTER 8

Where was she? It wasn't her bed. Whatever she was lying on was warm and hard. Hearing a low snore popped her eyes wide open. At first, nothing was in focus. It's what she got for sleeping in her contacts. The room was dimly lit, just the hint of light coming in under the curtains, so it couldn't be too late. When her eyes finally focused, she recognized the white dress shirt. Chase. What was he doing in bed with her? Then the brain fuzziness cleared and she remembered she was at Mick's house.

Sliding her arms across his chest, she hoped she didn't wake him. She'd prefer to slide out of bed and brush her teeth before talking to him.

That's when she saw remnants of her makeup on his shirt. Embarrassing. That's when the whole night came racing back, and she cringed. She'd gotten drunk with Mick, or she'd gotten drunk while Mick stayed sober was more like it. Then she'd begged Chase to stay with her. Double, ugh. That wasn't the way to keep her distance.

"How are you feeling?" So much for brushing her teeth first.

"Okay. Good. Did I wake you?"

"After all the years as a SEAL I don't sleep very soundly. Seems you can take the man out of the SEALs but not the SEAL out of the man."

"I'm sorry."

"Don't be. I enjoyed having you in my arms."

"Yeah, well, don't get used to it." She needed to reset the boundaries she'd blown out of the water last night. It was why she rarely drank except when she was alone with her friends. They were safe, and if she ever said or did anything off the wall, it stayed between them. She couldn't remember most of what she'd said to Chase the night before. That was never a good sign.

"I won't, at least not yet." She could hear the grin in his voice, but she could imagine how bad she looked and there was no way she was meeting his eyes. She needed to hold on to whatever remnants of pride she could.

"Do you know what time it is?" He shifted beneath her.

"Six forty-five. It's early. You've only had about three hours of sleep. Are you sure you don't want to try for more?"

"I don't think I can, but you go ahead. You got less that I did. I'll just get up."

"I'm awake. I'm used to getting up early. I'm usually running on the beach by five a.m."

"You run at five? You are crazy. That's too early for anyone to be awake."

"No, it's habit. Ten miles every morning when I'm home. If I'm on assignment, I still try to do it, but it's harder to find the time depending on what I'm working on."

"That makes sense. Are you going to go for a run now?"

"I'll skip it this morning, I can always go

later on. But I could go for a cup of coffee. How about I make some?"

"Sounds great, thank you." He rolled away from her and sat on the edge of the bed. After running his hands through his hair, he put on his shoes. "Still take it the same?" he asked with a smile.

"Yup, two sugars and some milk or cream or whatever they have. I'm easy." He smiled again. Damn, he was sexy, and she couldn't help admiring his butt in his dress slacks as he climbed the stairs.

He'd slept in his clothing and still looked like he should be on the cover of GQ. She was afraid to look in the bathroom mirror and see what a disaster she was. Especially since she just remembered the nightmare. Gee, Faith, home run girlfriend. You probably look like something left over from the zombie apocalypse.

Jumping out of bed, she almost fell as her legs got twisted in the quilt. So much for graceful. Small favors that he was already upstairs and missed that moment of poise. Good thing she didn't do that on stage last night. Until that point, she'd managed to forget the whole mess from yesterday. But there it was in all its spectacular glory. Bright pink flashing neon letters saying welcome to Faith's screwed up life.

This morning they'd have to figure out what to do. Hopefully, the partial license plate number Chase got would help to figure out who the man was who had been wreaking havoc with her life.

Pulling clothes out of one of her suitcases, she grabbed her makeup bag and headed to the bathroom. A quick shower would help put things in perspective or at least make her presentable.

By the time she emerged from the bathroom, Chase was back with their coffee. He'd made the bed and was sitting in one of the chairs typing away on his laptop. Where had that come from?

"Feel better?"

"Much. And thank you for the coffee."

"You're welcome. I figured I'd check some things while I was waiting for you. I forgot to bring in my bag from your car last night, so I grabbed it while I was upstairs. It's easier to research on the computer than the phone."

"It's crazy how people use their phones for everything. If I had to do all my work on the

phone, I'd be blind." She was too chatty. It
wasn't like her. Nerves were not her friend.
Where was her usual persona? It was always
there when she'd needed it, and she'd keep it
wrapped around her like a cloak. Maybe she
was off from the wine. Or maybe it was
having slept in his arms. At least, she knew
they'd only slept since they'd both been fully
dressed.

"Do you want to talk about yesterday?"

She'd just taken a sip of her coffee and
almost choked when he asked. Did she want to
talk about yesterday? Hell no. Of course she
didn't want to talk about it. Wait, what part of
yesterday? It didn't matter. They had to talk
about it. There was the stalker crazy stuff, and
their feelings for each other. She couldn't deny it
even if she wanted to. But it didn't mean she
had to give in to them either. She could be
strong. She'd done it before and she'd been
miserable too. So much for time healing
everything.

"What part of yesterday?"

"Either, but I was thinking of your stalker
issue." Whew. Not going to be pleasant but definitely the safer of the two options.

"Okay, unless you want to wait for Max and Mick?"

"I have a few questions if you're up for it."

"Go ahead."

"Do you remember your nightmare?"

"Yes, I do. It scared the heck out of me."

"Your subconscious is a powerful thing. You know that better than most people But for you to dream about him almost touching you makes me wonder if you know who it is."

"I don't."

"Wait, hear me out. Okay?"

She didn't want to, but if it would help she had to try. She took another sip of coffee and nodded.

"Let's go over the things we know for sure."

"Okay, but if we wait for Max and Mick, we won't have to do this twice."

"You don't have to wait, we're up. Why don't you come upstairs? Mick is whipping up some pancakes as we speak," Max said from the stairs.

"Homemade pancakes? Hell yeah." Apparently Chase was a sucker for homemade pancakes. She'd have to file that away for possible later use. If she'd needed proof that the way to a man's heart was through his stomach she had the verification right there.

"Great, we'll be right up."

"Oh and whoever made the coffee, thank you," Max said as he disappeared up the stairs.

He didn't want to push her, but if there was something in her subconscious that might help them figure out who it was, he had to try. They'd used the process a number of times with excellent results.

The aroma of pancakes and bacon made his stomach growl. Faith wasn't the only one who hadn't eaten dinner the night before. With all the stuff going on at CC's he'd never gotten around to ordering any food.

"Morning."

"Good morning. I hope you both slept well?" Mick's intonation told him he'd better not have done anything he shouldn't have. It was almost like having parents checking up on you. They were doing it out of love for Faith, and worry that he'd hurt her. But only time would prove to them all that he wouldn't.

"Yes, I did. Thank you for letting me stay here," Faith said as she poured another cup of coffee.

"And no hangover?"

"No. I'm good. Well as much as I could be under the circumstances."

"Thank you, too. I know what you're thinking, and yes, I behaved myself."

"Glad to hear it," Max remarked with a grin. "I wouldn't want to have to take you out back and beat you to a pulp this early."

"Gee, thanks. I appreciate it."

"You're welcome." If they'd been children, they'd probably have stuck their tongues out at each other. The silliness was fabricated though, and all for Faith's benefit. It was obvious she was incredibly stressed.

"Breakfast is served." Mick put a plate of pancakes and bacon on the table. They dug in like they hadn't eaten in years. No one said a thing until the plates were wiped clean. The food helped to take care of the headache he'd had when he woke up, hopefully for good.

Faith helped Mick clear the table and do the dishes while the men went into the living room to talk. Chase's team had emailed him about the car and come up with a few options. The best part, there were no records of cars having been stolen with that description or partial. They were on the right track.

He hoped it meant that her months of hell were finally coming to an end. She should have told her friends sooner, but if she had, he wouldn't be there with her now. She hadn't been physically hurt and was back in his life. He'd have to say it was a good thing on both counts.

The women came in as Max and Chase were discussing the results of his team at Eagle Security & Protection. Rock, his computer guy, managed to find things that didn't seem possible and he'd send them four names. Hopefully, Faith would recognize one of them.

If she didn't, it might take a bit longer, but they would figure it out, of that he had no doubt. What they weren't sharing with Mick and Faith was that Riot and his team were checking out each of the men. Rock had gotten a good start, but he was still working on their detailed background checks.

"Okay, so Rock came up with some names of men who might own the car I saw at your house last night. We don't know for sure that it was your stalker, but it's a likely option. Normal traffic doesn't behave that way," Chase said. He knew in his gut it was the stalker. Besides, as soon as he ran outside, the car had taken off.

"Okay. I guess you're hoping one of them sounds familiar to me, right?"

"Yes. And even if you do recognize one of them, we still need evidence before we can go to the police. But we'll be able to keep an eye on him."

"Are you okay," Mick asked Faith, concern evident on her face.

"Yes. I'm just frustrated. If Rock was able to come up with names so fast, just think if I'd come to you guys sooner. This could have been over a long time ago." Chase didn't know what to say to make it better. What she said was true.

"It's okay. We'll get this taken care of, and then you can put it behind you, right?"

"True. Thank you." Faith took a deep breath and seemed to center herself. There was his doc, the one he'd fallen in love with. When she met his eyes he winked. She smiled slightly and nodded her head. "Okay. what are the names?"

"First name is Roger Benning? Does he sound familiar?"

"No. Not even a little."

"Harold MacPhail?"

She hesitated and thought about it, but then shook her head no.

"How about Frank Peters?"

"Definitely no."

"Are you sure? You're around a lot of people. Remember, it doesn't have to be a patient, it could be another doctor or even a volunteer at the VA or on base. Hell, it could be someone you come into contact with at the grocery store."

Neither of them thought the last option was much of a possibility. It was probably someone she saw on a daily basis.

"I know, and I'm trying. But I don't know anyone named Frank Peters."

Chase was frustrated, he couldn't help it. He'd been so sure it was one of these guys and now there was only one name left. If she didn't recognize this one they'd be back at square one. He'd wondered how many nights she'd woken up terrified from the same dream as she'd had last night.

"Okay. The last name on the list is Melvin Iverson."

They didn't need to wait for her answer, the look on her face was enough. There was no doubt she'd recognized his name.

CHAPTER 9

Could it be Melvin? It made sense in a weird way. He was a doctor at the VA Hospital in San Diego and he'd been referring patients to her group sessions since the beginning of the year. He'd always seemed a little off, but she'd chalked it up to overwork. They all had their hands full over there. It was one of the reasons she'd started volunteering. Her colleagues on base thought she was crazy that she had enough with her regular patients. She understood their point of view, but these men and women gave everything for their country, and if she could make a difference in their lives, she was going to do it.

But Dr. Melvin Iverson was a definite possibility. Now that she thought about it, she remembered asking about him when she'd first met him. No one had known much about him since he'd transferred from a VA hospital in Washington a few months prior. But if it was him, did he have access to the base too since the notes first showed up there?

They'd had coffee a couple of times, but she wouldn't call them dates. Mostly they talked about work, and how her volunteer sessions were going. Her training told her it didn't matter what she thought, it only mattered what was in his mind. If he was her stalker, then his mind was a dark and scary place.

"What are you thinking, Faith? Do you know him?" Chase asked. His voice brought her back to reality and the three sets of eyes waiting for her answer.

"Yes, I know him, unless there is more than one Melvin Iverson. He's a doctor at the VA Hospital in San Diego. I met him when I started volunteering over there. In fact, he was the person who helped me get the group sessions started. But I don't think he has access to the base. So, it can't be him, right?"

"When was this?"

She had to think. Craptastic. "About seven months ago."

"Coincidence? I think not," Chase responded. She had to agree with him, it was looking increasingly like Melvin was her stalker, but she wasn't ready to convict him. It would be too easy.

"Maybe, but it doesn't mean it's him."

"No, but it's good enough for us to dig deeper. In the meantime, be careful around him. Don't give him any reason to think you suspect him," Chase said, and Max nodded in agreement.

"But, won't it be better if he knows I know? Isn't that what he's looking for? Validation of his feelings?"

Chase grinned. "The doctor is in the house. But no, you don't want to give him any encouragement. He's escalating enough on his own."

"Okay."

"When is your next group session?" Mick asked.

"Monday. We meet on Monday, Wednesday and Fridays at four p.m."

"That doesn't give us much time," Chase mused. "I'll call Riot and let him know we have a new direction. Then I'll follow up with Rock and see if he's been able to dig up anything else on Dr. Iverson."

"If it is him, how did he leave me notes on base?"

"I don't know. But we'll find out soon enough if he has access."

"Aren't you glad I made you tell Chase?" Mick said with a gentle smile. She was trying to reassure her, and Faith appreciated it. For the first time in a while, she thought it might turn out okay. She'd been lucky he hadn't hurt her. Hopefully, they'd be able to stop him before he killed anything else.

They spent the next few hours planning and investigating. By the end of the day, they'd know if he was the one. Faith wasn't sure how they'd know for sure without proof, but she trusted them. Chase had been by her side all day and it was like he was her security blanket. Except whenever they touched every nerve ending burned with desire, she'd forgotten existed. She was drawn to him like a moth to a flame. If she got too close would she be burned?

By the evening she realized he'd been right, all their time separated hadn't changed a thing.

The feelings that had grown over the months they'd known each other had been rekindled and the flame was burning brighter than ever. It wouldn't matter if she 'allowed' him into her life again, he was already there, had been there, and had only been hidden by sheer force of will. When he left this time, she didn't want to think about the shattered pieces of her heart he'd leave behind.

She slept in his arms again that night, and once again she had the nightmare, but this time she saw Melvin's face.

They woke to a beautiful sunny day. She hoped it was a good omen for things to come. The plan was in motion. Chase had called the rental car company the day before and let them know about this car. What he hadn't told her was that all his tires had been slashed. She didn't have to try to guess who'd done that. But now that Chase was in the picture would Melvin, if it was him, turn his wrath on him instead of the helpless furry animals? She couldn't bear the thought of being the cause of anyone or anything else getting hurt, but especially not Chase.

"Hey, if you keep biting that lip, you're going to leave a permanent mark," Chase said as he gently touched her lower lip where it had been between her teeth. It was a bad habit and most of the time she didn't realize she was doing it.

"You're right. I need a distraction. Just waiting around until tomorrow for something to happen is driving me out of my mind." She needed to get out and do something, rehearse her new act, walk on the beach, anything other than sit and wait. Patience was never one of her strong suits.

"We can't have that," he said with a big smile. God, she loved his mouth.

"I can pick up a new rental in about an hour. They took care of the other one yesterday. The only hitch is they need me to file a police report. How would you like to take a drive to the station?"

"You mean you're going to let me out in public? You bet. I'll drive you. I'd go anywhere to get out of the house." Faith was thrilled to have an excuse to get out of the house. She loved Max and Mick and appreciated that they were letting her hide out in their home. But being told not to go out was too much like when she was in one of the group homes growing up.

"What are you going to tell them?" Max asked from the doorway.

"That I was visiting Faith. When I left to go home, I found the tires like that."

"That should work."

"Yeah. I'd rather keep the police out of this until we have something concrete to share. Getting them involved now will just make things more complicated."

"Exactly."

Mick decided a barbeque would be a good distraction for Faith and invited Syn and Honey, and Riot's team. After they took care of the police report, they were free until five p.m. It was as close to a date as he could hope for and his goal was to help her relax and smile. The "real" dates would come later, after this mess was resolved, and she was safe.

He'd been contemplating opening an office

on the west coast. Maybe this was the push he'd needed. It might be enough to get Steele to leave the Willow Haven Police Department and join ESP. Then he could run the Florida office, and Chase could stay in California, close to Faith.

Their first stop was the police station. It was almost empty, and he made his report and they got out of there in less than an hour. Rather than pick up his car right away, he suggested that they grab some lunch.

"Any preferences?"

"Something light since I know what the barbeques are like. There will be enough food to feed an army or maybe I should say three SEAL teams. If it's meat, it will be there, and the women always bring lots of side dishes."

"Sounds like perfection. I know a little place downtown. Hopefully, it's still there. They used to have great artisan sandwiches."

"A sandwich sounds good."

The café was where he remembered and offered indoor and outdoor seating. He'd have preferred to sit outside in the beautiful weather but inside was the safer option. There would be plenty of time for patio lunches in their future.

The weather was usually perfect in San Diego and was one of the things he missed. Florida had good weather too, but the constant humidity reminded him of his missions in the South American jungles.

While they waited for their sandwiches, he asked how she'd gotten started with burlesque.

"I was looking for a way to unwind, find a release from work, and to distract me from thinking about you."

"From me?"

"Yes, you. I found an ad in the paper for dance classes. It wasn't until I showed up the first evening that I realized the classes were in burlesque. Apparently, I missed the fine print. Since I was there, I gave it a chance, and really enjoyed it. It helped me forget about everything and find some peace for my heart. Hence my choice of name."

"Riven Heart. I wondered about the reasoning behind that. I'm sorry I caused you so much pain. It's the last thing I wanted. I was really messed up back then, and I had no business trying to pull you down with me."

"It wasn't your fault. I'm the professional. I should have seen what was happening, but my own feelings got in the way. It wasn't something I expected, but you were—are—irresistible. You have no reason to apologize for anything."

"I'm sure Mick would disagree. Hell. I disagree. I have everything to apologize for. You could have lost everything."

"But I didn't. And I learned a new skill because of it." Faith grinned. She really was remarkable, he'd made a mess of things, and she was trying to reassure him.

"How about we agree to disagree?" When she nodded, he continued. "How did lessons turn into a burlesque troupe with, what were their names, Honey Pot and Syn something?"

"Honey Potter and Syn LaRue. We met in class and hit it off. They've been friends forever and were so funny. I needed some fun in my life."

It was his turn to nod. Everyone needed fun in their life. Too many people ignored that fact, and it was how they got into trouble. There's a reason they say 'all work and no play makes Jack a dull boy.' Except it turned into depression or worse, and he had first hand knowledge.

Their food arrived. It looked as wonderful as

he'd remembered. "This is really good. I'll have to come back here."

"I'm surprised you didn't know about it."

"I'm so busy, I don't get out much except for rehearsals and shows. Between my patients and running the support group, I'm lucky I remember to throw in a microwave dinner when I get home."

"You need some downtime, baby."

"Oh yeah? I suppose you're going to tell me that you take tons of time off?" She had him there, but it was different for him, wasn't it?

"No, I'm not, and you're right. I need to have more fun in my life too. I'm glad you found the dancing and your friends."

"Me too."

"I've never seen a burlesque show. You blew me out of the water. It was the sexiest thing I've ever seen."

Color bathed her cheeks, and she looked down at her plate. He wasn't trying to embarrass her, just to pay her a compliment. "I didn't mean to make you uncomfortable."

"You didn't, okay you did. But it shouldn't. How can I do this and get embarrassed when people compliment me? I'll chalk it up to still getting used to it. We haven't been performing very long. Most of the time I'm in costume and anonymous when people say something."

"Is that why you wear the mask?"

"I started wearing it because Coronado is small, much smaller when you have a secret you want to keep. There aren't a lot of places to perform either, so when Mick agreed to give it a shot I decided it would be best to hide my identity. I'm sure my patients wouldn't be distracted at all if they saw their doctor performing half-naked on stage and then had an appointment for therapy." She laughed, and it was like a breath of fresh air. Pure, sweet, happy. He was head over heels for her. It got more intense with every moment they spent together.

He'd planned to take her to the beach, but instead they sat and talked all afternoon, drinking iced tea and laughing. He told her about his new company and some of his crew. She told him funny stories about her dancing, and some really embarrassing wardrobe malfunctions during her first few performances.

Too soon it was time to pick up his car and head back to Mick's house. He hated that the afternoon had to end. She'd been relaxed and happy, and he'd intentionally steered the conversation to happier topics. But heading back to Mick's would bring the tension back. He hoped they'd be able to get this wrapped up by tomorrow but it wasn't a guarantee. After they took care of her stalker, he intended to do what he could to convince her they were meant to be together. He planned on staying until she agreed.

The barbecue was everything she said it would be. It was great hanging out with a team again. For the first time it didn't hurt. Even seeing Riot interacting with his new team only stung a little. Chase even got to meet Ariana, the woman he was seeing. She was a cute little thing, feisty, and would keep him on his toes. He was glad he'd made the decision to stop by Coronado after his job, it had been good for him in more ways than one.

CHAPTER 10

It was close to eleven by the time everyone left, and they got everything cleaned up. Max had been gone for most of it, having to take care of CC's with Mick staying for the party.

"You don't get much alone time with Max, do you?" Faith asked as they were putting the last of the dishes away.

"During the day we do. Our schedule is backward from everyone else's. We work nights and sleep until mid-morning then have our days. I don't even notice it I've been doing it for so long."

"I'm curious why name it CC's Saloon?"

"People have been asking me that for almost

as long as I've been open. I like having some secrets." Mick laughed. "Maybe one of these days but for now it's too much fun keeping everyone guessing."

Faith grinned. You can't fault a girl for trying. She hadn't expected Mick to tell her either. "You and Max have been so wonderful to me, I don't know how I'll ever repay you."

"No worries, honey. You are family to us. It's what families do for one another." Faith's eyes teared up. Her experience with family had been nothing like this.

"Thank you. I still want you to know how much I appreciate it. And I won't mention to anyone that you and Max are living together."

"I wasn't worried about that. But if they find out, it doesn't matter either. I just like to have some privacy."

"I get it. Especially now that mine was stolen by my stalker. I'm still not sure it's Melvin."

"I am," Chase said as he stepped into the kitchen.

"What did you find out?" Mick asked before she had a chance.

"Guess who has a badge and can come and go on base as much as he wants?"

"Iverson?"

"Yeah. He's in the Naval reserves and consults on some cases. I'm surprised you never ran into him."

"Me too," Faith replied. It was weird, she should have unless he purposely avoided her. None of this made sense. "I feel like we're missing a piece of the puzzle. What triggered his behavior now?"

"Who knows? It could have been anything, you of all people should know that. But don't worry, baby. Now that we know about it, we'll be able to track him down."

Nodding, Faith finished drying the last dish and put it in the cabinet. Something wasn't right, but she didn't know how to put her concerns into words. Hopefully Chase was right, and it would all be over tomorrow.

"Chase, are you staying here tonight?" He looked between her and Mick. The yearning in his eyes pleaded for her to say yes, but she knew he'd wait for her to respond.

"It's fine with me," Faith answered as she threw the wet dishtowel at his head. He caught it without missing a beat.

"Then yes, I'm staying."

"Good. I can head over to the bar and I won't have to worry about our girl being alone. I want to check and see how it's going there." Faith wanted to tell her she didn't need a babysitter, but she knew her heart was in the right place. If this stalking thing taught her anything, it was that she had to learn to let people into her life and not just on the surface.

"Don't you mean check on Max?"

"Don't you get sassy with me. I will kick your butt, ex-SEAL or not."

"Yes, ma'am," Chase said with a laugh. Mick wagged her finger in his face.

"What did I tell you about that ma'am crap?"

"Sorry." He tried to look contrite but instead it cracked them up.

"You two be good. Don't do anything I wouldn't."

"That doesn't leave much does it," Chase called after her. Mick was laughing as she went out the front door.

As soon as the door closed behind her, Chase took Faith into his arms. "Are you sure you're okay?

"I just keep wondering what made him do

this. Why me? Was I too nice? Did I make him think I liked him romantically? What did I do to trigger his behavior if it is him? I'm still not convinced he's the one."

"I'll play devil's advocate. If it's not him then do you have any other ideas who it might be? The evidence is pretty damning. The black car, the access to you at the VA and on base, being able to figure out where you live. He'd have access to those records at the hospital."

"I know, but…"

"You don't like to see the worst in anyone. It's what makes you a wonderful doctor but more, it makes you an amazing person."

"If I'm so wonderful why didn't I see it?"

"Because you're too close to the situation."

"Maybe. I just…" Before she could finish her thought, Chase's cell rang.

"It's Rock, why don't you get ready for bed and I'll be down as soon as I check the locks."

"Okay." He dropped a kiss on her forehead and hugged her before he let her go. Maybe Rock would have more information and remove her doubts for good. The last thing she wanted on her conscience was to accuse an innocent man. It would ruin him.

Trying to figure this out was like trying to unravel a knotted ball of yarn or doing a puzzle that was missing a few pieces. It frustrated the crap out of her and she didn't like it. Control. She thrived on it probably from her lack of it when she was growing up.

Sighing, she grabbed a nightshirt from her suitcase and went to take a shower. The hot water helped to ease the tension until she thought about Chase. Then a different kind of tenseness stole over her. He was everything she remembered and more. When he held her, she wanted to melt, it was only sheer force of will that kept her on her feet instead of becoming a puddle at his feet.

Desire, longing, yearning, whatever it was, she had it bad. Her analytical mind told her it was a gut reaction to fear. Her emotions were going haywire, between the stress and fear and then the desire, she didn't know which way was up. How could she want him so badly? She'd tell her patients that they needed to take a step back, think about what they were feeling, before making any sudden changes in their lives. Stress and fear were powerful motivators but not a good enough reason for a relationship.

Then her heart reminded her that she felt this way before all of this happened, before the stalking, before he left town because she pushed him away. It was the right thing to do then, but now?

The steam from her shower floated from under the bathroom door. He didn't think Mick had a sauna in there, so she must have the temperature way up. Was she trying to scald herself?

Knocking on the door, he yelled, "Are you okay?" The water stopped a few seconds later.

"I'm good. I like to take really hot showers."

He rolled his eyes and mumbled, "I can see that." He'd have to remember that she would try to burn his ass when he finally got her in the shower with him. He liked it hot but not so much he melted.

When they'd been out running around, they'd stopped by his hotel and picked up a few things just in case, and now he was glad he had. I really didn't want to sleep in his clothing again, but he would for her. He'd been tempted to check out, but he didn't want to push his luck.

The door to the bathroom opened releasing a cloud of heat and steam that fogged up his reading glasses. Faith appeared out of the mist like a goddess. Instead of sexy lingerie as he'd hoped, she wore a nightshirt that said *I am the coffee queen*. It cracked him up.

"What's so funny?"

"Just my overactive imagination. I envisioned you wearing some sexy little nothing, but instead the coffee queen appears in a puff of smoke."

"What? Not sexy enough for you?"

"You will always be sexy enough."

"Right," she answered with a smirk. He still had a lot of convincing to do but he'd take it as slow as she needed.

"It's true, baby. One of these days I hope you believe me." She flashed him a glorious smile and turned around. At first, he thought she was going to moon him, but it was to read the back of her shirt, which said *you can't touch this*.

He laughed so hard he almost choked. "You are way too cute."

"Cute? I'm not ten, I'm a grown woman. You don't call grown women cute."

"Sorry, sorry." He was still laughing about her sleep shirt. Getting up from the chair, he held open his arms, letting the choice be hers. He craved the feel of her body against his, to touch her, to kiss her. "I really am sorry. I won't use cute anymore. How does beautiful, delicious, precious, work?"

"They work just fine," she answered as she walked into his waiting arms. What she did next surprised the hell out of him. As soon as his arms closed around her waist, she pulled his head down and kissed him. Gentle, almost shy at first, but his moan must have made her brave because she slid her tongue along the edge of his lips.

It was all the invitation he needed. He lifted her and carried her over to the bed. He reminded himself he had to take it slow. Lying down with her on the bed, he pulled her on top of him, giving her the control. Then he took her mouth in a blistering kiss, filled with all the longing he'd kept stored away.

The scent of cherry blossoms wafted over him as her chestnut-brown hair fell around their faces like a veil. It was the scent he'd tried to recall so many times over the years, but now he'd never forget it. She tasted like mint as her tongue slid between his lips to duel with his.

She had to feel his erection pressing against her. Every time she shifted, she rubbed against it. "Baby, you're killing me."

"Oh, I'm sorry." She shifted on top of him and he groaned again.

"No, don't move."

"I didn't mean to hurt you."

"You're not hurting me, it feels good. Too good."

"I'm out of practice."

"Me too, I haven't been with a woman since before my last mission."

"Seriously? In all this time…"

"I never wanted anyone else after I met you. I'm not saying I didn't take care of things on my own. But there's been no other women."

She sat up and balanced on his hips, putting all her weight exactly where it felt the best. He was dying. It took all his control not to move underneath her.

"I haven't been with anyone either." He'd wondered, it wouldn't have surprised him to find out she was a virgin. It meant he'd have to take it even more slowly.

"We don't have to do anything else. Can stop right here. No pressure." Her mischievous smile should have warned him. She leaned back and slid her hand along this pulsing dick. He closed his eyes and tried to think about anything that wasn't Faith. He was going to embarrass himself for sure.

"And if I don't want to stop?"

Yes, she was determined to kill him. "I don't want to rush you or for you to have any regrets. You're in a highly stressful situation, you haven't been sleeping, or eating… No don't give me that look, I've been around you since Friday night I know exactly how much food you've had."

"You're not my babysitter…"

"No, I'm not. I want to be your lover, your best friend, your husband. And because of that I don't want to do anything as stupid as I did before."

"My husband?" Of course, of all he said she'd point out that one. Not that it wasn't true, but he really needed to work on controlling what came out of his mouth.

CHAPTER 11

Holy crap on a cracker. Of all the things she expected it wasn't that. He didn't *actually* ask her to marry him, but the intent was there. What was she doing? He was right, she wasn't herself, the last few months had taken their toll. But why couldn't this be her, she'd spent most of her life afraid to trust, afraid to take chances, and where had it gotten her. Even without dating she'd managed to attract a stalker. What kind of crappy luck was that?

"I need to learn how to keep my mouth shut around you. I have no control."

"Just around me?"

"Yes, just you. I'm fine around everyone else.

But you… it's just different. Like all my training goes right out the window."

"That's kind of flattering. Dangerous for you but flattering." Smiling, she rocked back and forth over his erection.

"Thanks," Chase said with a laugh and a groan. "Maybe we should table this discussion for now."

"Good idea. Then we can get back to the fun stuff." She thought his eyebrows were going to disappear into his hairline he looked so surprised. She liked playing the siren, burlesque dancing made her more comfortable with her sexuality.

"Are you sure you want this? Because it will be hard as hell for me to stop if you change your mind."

"I'm not a virgin. It's just been a long time."

"Then how about you stay where you are and take the lead. If you want to stop, it will be easier if you're in control."

"Really? You'd let me be in control?"

"Of course, baby. Why wouldn't I? It's about pleasure and making sure you're taken care of. It doesn't matter who's in control." Another surprise. She'd never expected her big, strong, domineering ex-SEAL to give up control in the bedroom or anywhere else. But he'd known exactly what she needed. The frisson of fear that had been lurking in the back of her mind dissipated like smoke in the wind.

"Thank you." She didn't want to talk anymore. She wanted to taste him, to feel him, to see all of him. To find out if her fantasies matched the reality that was Chase.

Opening the buttons on his dress shirt one at a time, she slowly revealed his chest like she was unwrapping a candy bar. She licked her lips in anticipation and he groaned. But this time she knew she wasn't hurting him. Hopefully, her inexperience wouldn't ruin things for them, but for once she was beyond caring.

With his shirt open and pushed to his sides, she slid her fingertips over his muscles, and circled his nipples. Leaning forward, she ran her tongue over the tip of the hard nub. Then she licked the other one as she slid her fingers through the light sprinkling of hair on his chest. There wasn't an extra ounce on him. He'd kept in shape not that she'd expected any different.

Sitting back, she pulled her nightshirt over her head and watched the expression on his face. He'd seen her in her burlesque costume but naked was different. She was proud of her curvy figure, she'd never wanted to be one of the skinny women always worried about their size zero body. Although she'd lost some weight the last few months, she still had plenty of curves.

"Holy mother of God, you're gorgeous."

"I'm just an ordinary woman."

"There is nothing ordinary about you, baby. May I touch?"

"Yes, please." She'd expected him to go for her breasts but instead he pulled her down onto his chest. The heat of his body against her sent shivers down her spine. She squirmed against him, and he moaned before taking her mouth in a passionate kiss.

Leaving her lips, he slid his tongue along her throat and down to her chest. He teased her nipples the way she'd teased his making her moan.

"Let me know if anything makes you feel uncomfortable or hurts."

"I will."

"Promise me, because I will stop if you want, you just have to say it."

"I promise. Now shut up and go back to what you were doing." She felt him grin against her as his tongue continued its exploration of her breasts.

Yearning for more, she climbed over to the side and unbuckled his belt, then unzipped his pants. There was only one layer of fabric between them. His erection twitched against her fingers as she slid them down his rigid cock.

"You're wearing entirely too much clothing. Especially since I'm wearing nothing."

"Agreed. Shall I do something about it?"

"Definitely. Or I'll rip it off you and you'll have to replace it all." His grin was priceless but seeing him naked in his full glory took her breath away. The boy in college was nothing compared to the man standing in front of her. Chase was one hundred percent red-blooded male from head to toe.

"Dear God. You're like a Greek statue."

"Your Greek statue." And then there was no more talking. He climbed onto the bed and laid on his back. She learned every inch of his body starting with his lips and slowly working her way down to his dick.

It seemed huge, not that she had a lot to

compare it to, but he would definitely be more than a mouthful. Her first taste wasn't what she'd expected, musky and a little salty. Taking another lick, she circled his head with her tongue watching the expressions on his face. Then sucked the head into her mouth. His hips arched, and his fists clenched in the sheets, but he didn't stop her. As promised, he let her do what she wanted. She must have pushed a bit too far because in the space of a breath he'd flipped her over onto her back.

"I need to taste you." Before she could say a word, he'd moved between her legs and showed her what it was like to be worshipped. His tongue, and teeth licked and nibbled her clit, and slid into her lapping the juices. It was unlike anything she'd felt before. Her body clenched, and she couldn't control her hips as they arched against his mouth needing more. And then every nerve ending lit up as her first orgasm crashed around her like the stars were falling from the sky. She'd barely regained her breath before he brought her there again until she was a boneless puddle of orgasmic bliss.

He got up. She wanted to object, but she

didn't have the energy. Then she realized he'd just went to get a condom.

"I want to make love to you. Will you let me?"

All she could manage was a whisper, but it was enough. If she'd thought she'd been to the moon and back before, making love to Chase was like shooting into the Milky Way and back. She wasn't sure she'd ever be able to move again.

"I love you, baby. You're an amazing woman."

"I love you," Faith whispered as she fell asleep.

Chase couldn't take his eyes away from her. She looked so peaceful. After she'd fallen asleep, he'd used a warm washcloth on her, hoping it would help with any soreness in the morning. He prayed that she wouldn't have any regrets. He'd wanted this for so long and it was so much better than he'd dreamed.

He could have walked on water at that point and was just about to climb into bed next to her when reality came flooding back when his cell phone chirped with a message. He'd completely forgotten about Rock's call earlier and his text to Riot. Seeing Faith wiped everything else out of his thoughts. He needed to keep on top of this until the fucker was caught and couldn't hurt her any longer.

The phone chirped again. Typing in his code, he saw two message one from Rock and one from Riot. Neither of them was good news. He didn't want to make a call and risk waking up Faith, so he replied to their messages and signed into his computer to read the information Rock had sent.

Riot's information was infuriating. Somehow Iverson had slipped through their hands. His team had been taking turns watching him. But he got away. They were doing their best to locate him, but he was in the wind.

Iverson had figured out they made him, it was the only possible reason he'd run. But that he'd managed to slip past a SEAL team made him even more dangerous. There was no way he was going to let Faith out of his sight. He wished they had more concrete evidence to take to the police, but everything they'd found was circumstantial or obtained in ways they couldn't share.

Closing his computer after reading Rock's latest intel, he shut off the light and climbed into bed. He pulled Faith against his side and he'd swear she purred with contentment. Praying she'd sleep through the night, he kissed her on the forehead and stared at the ceiling for a long time before finally falling asleep.

CHAPTER 12

W aking up in Chase's arms with the memories of the night before had to be the best thing ever. She wished she could just stay tucked against his side and forget about the rest of the world. But it wasn't possible. As soon as she'd opened her eyes, it all came flooding back.

It was Monday. Her calendar was full and after that she had her group session at the VA hospital. She was bound to run into Melvin somewhere. Especially after what he'd done on Friday.

"Morning, baby. How are you?" Chase's sleep-roughened voice vibrated against her head where it rested on his chest. She'd been trying to stay calm and not wake him.

"Yes, I did. How about you?"

"Yup. I'm happy you didn't have any nightmares. Are you okay? No regrets?"

Regrets? About last night? How could he even think that? "Absolutely not. Last night was one of the best nights of my life." She could feel his relief as his body relaxed into the bed and she smiled. She didn't want to get up, wanted to hold on to the little cocoon of happiness as long as possible. But it wasn't to be. No sooner had the thoughts formed in her head when Chase's phone rang.

"Ugh, they're starting early. Sorry, baby." He kissed her forehead and rolled out of bed to grab his phone. "I'll go make some coffee so you can get ready. Be right back."

Was he trying to keep her from hearing his conversation? From the look on his face as he headed up the stairs it wasn't good news. Yeah, reality was back full force and the legion of doom was resting heavily on her shoulders. There wasn't a shower hot enough in existence to help her relax. It made her even more thankful for the time with Chase. She'd always have those memories to cherish whatever the future brought.

After her shower, she'd expected to find him waiting for her, but he hadn't come back downstairs. Pulling out one of her suits, she dressed, put on her makeup, and headed upstairs. She needed coffee and a lot of it. Their escapades had kept them up late but for the first time in weeks she hadn't had a nightmare.

"What do you mean you still haven't found him? What the hell? No, she'll never agree to that. We'll have to come up with a different option. Okay, call me when you can." Chase was pissed off as he disconnected the call. They still hadn't been able to locate Iverson. How he could have disappeared off the face of the earth was beyond all of them.

He dumped his phone, his car, and no one knew where he was. Riot had broken into his house and it was deserted. Too bad they didn't believe he'd left town. He was coming for Faith. Chase knew it with every bone in his body. And he was just as determined that he wouldn't succeed.

"What's going on?"

Damn, he hadn't heard her come up the stairs. It was just the two of them. Max and Mick were still sleeping since they worked most of the night. "How about some coffee first?"

"Nope, don't pull that. I'm a big girl, just tell me." She was right.

"Iverson gave Riot's team the slip. We don't know where he is."

"That's good though, right? He probably figured out we were on to him and he left town."

"That's one scenario. But we don't think that's the case. We think he's hiding out waiting for his chance to get to you." He would have given anything not to tell her, but she needed to know and as his words sank in the color drained from her face. "Baby, sit down. You look like you're going to pass out."

"I'm okay. Really. But I'll take that coffee now."

He poured them each a cup and sat at the table. He reached for her hand and wasn't surprised when it was as cold as ice. When he got ahold of that mother fucker, he'd make him pay for what he'd done to her. He'd picked the wrong woman.

"I think you should call out from work today. It would be safer if you stayed here."

"I can't do that. I have patients. They need me." He'd expected that answer, but he'd had to try.

"At least cancel the group session at the VA tonight?"

"We'll see. I'll see if one of the other doctors can cover for me tonight. But if I can't find a fill in, I have to go. They count on me."

"I know, but if something happens, they won't have you either." He hated to be that blunt, but she had to face it, she was in danger.

Her eyes were huge, and her pupils fully dilated when she met his eyes. She was scared but there was that iron will in there too. She wouldn't give in, so he'd have to make sure she stayed safe even if it meant sticking by her side all day, every day until they caught him.

"Chase, I understand. I do. But I'm not going to let him win. I don't know what I did to cause this, but I have to see it through. I will not go into hiding, it will just prolong the inevitable.

If he can't find me, he'll hurt someone else to get to me. Have you thought of that? What if it's Honey or Syn, or Mick? Or you? I could never live with myself."

"I know. If you won't stay here, then you're going to have to deal with me shadowing you."

"Fine, but you have to stay outside when I have my appointments. I have to get going I have a really full calendar today."

"Finish your coffee and I'll pack us a lunch." He downed his coffee and gave her a kiss on the lips and put together a quick lunch for them. He would rather have taken her out but the less out in the open she was the better.

It had been crazy busy from the moment she got into her office. She sent Chase to go find Riot since he was making her crazy hanging around. It's not like anything would happen while she was on base. There were too many people around.

"Dr. Murdock?" She'd just gotten out her lunch when there was a knock on her office door. It was too early for her next patient.

"Yes?"

Petty Officer Shannon O'Brien opened her door. "I have a message for you."

"Thank you."

"Oh, and your next appointment canceled. Andrews was admitted this morning for complications from last month's surgery."

"Oh no. Can you find out what room he's in? I'll visit him later before I go to my group."

"Yes, ma'am." She'd never get used to being called ma'am. Sometimes she wished she'd joined the Navy. She often felt like an imposter, she helped them, but she wasn't truly one of them. The petty officer stepped out and closed the door after handing Faith the message.

It was from Chase. Why hadn't he called her? She'd even remembered to put it on her desk in case something came up, instead of leaving it in her purse. There weren't any messages or missed calls. Weird. Then she saw there was no signal. No wonder he called the main number to reach her.

Meet me at your house. Something came up. I'll explain when you get here.

. . .

Still no signal on her phone. With the cancela-
tion she should be able to make it to the house
and back before the next appointment. Grabbing her bag, she tossed her phone in and told
Shannon she had to run home but would be
back as soon as possible.

It looked like she'd gotten there first. She
wasn't sure if she should wait for Chase or head
in. It was daytime, and Chase asked her to meet
him there so why shouldn't she go in? The nail
holes in her front door made her want to throw
up, and she quickly averted her eyes to unlock
the door. The vision of the squirrels dripping
blood on her front stoop was still too new to
ignore. With a shudder, she stepped into her
house and shut the door behind her.

"I'm so glad you could make it."

At first, she didn't recognize the voice. Then
realization dawned on her. But before she could
figure out whether to run or attack, he hit her
over the head.

～

The pain in her head was excruciating. She hadn't even opened her eyes, and she was dizzy. She tried to feel where he'd hit her, but she couldn't move. Struggling to open her eyes, she blinked to clear her vision. She was in her bedroom. Why was she there? Then it started to come back. Melvin. He'd tricked her into leaving her office and was waiting for her. The last thing she remembered was the pain and then nothing, he must have hit her over the head. How had he gotten in? Not that it mattered. She'd played right into his hands.

"Welcome back, beloved. I'm sorry I had to hit you, but I couldn't risk you trying to get away. I've waited for such a long time for you. Longer than anyone else."

Anyone else? There'd been others? The icy fingers of fear closed around her heart. "I didn't know it was you." Keeping him talking seemed like a good idea. If she could stall long enough, maybe Chase would figure out where she was, or he could kill her, whichever came first. Because looking into his cold, dark eyes, all she could see was madness and was surprised he hadn't killed her yet.

"You should have. You're not stupid. When I

saw your first show, I was livid. You always acted so proper at the hospital, but then you strip for perfect strangers? It made me wonder if you were a whore in disguise."

There probably wasn't much use in explaining that burlesque wasn't the same as being a stripper. And she didn't want to address the whore comment. It was a word meant to incite, and she needed to keep him as calm as possible. "How many shows have you seen?"

"All of them. I would never miss the opportunity to see my beloved. Did you like the presents? I bet you were surprised."

"Yes, you could say that. Most men would have sent flowers or candy."

"I'm not most men," he roared. That was an understatement. *C'mon Faith, use your training. Maybe you can talk your way out of this mess.*

"I know, you're one of a kind. What I don't understand is why all the secrecy. Why not just talk to me at the hospital instead of leaving me notes?"

"I was trying to be romantic, to woo you." The guy had some heavy-duty relationship issues if he thought stalking equated to wooing. "Didn't you like the notes and gifts?"

"Yes, of course I did. Thank you for thinking of me."

"Then why didn't you answer me? I love you. You're mine. But I'm extremely disappointed in you. What are you doing with those SEALs? Don't you know they're just a bunch of man-whores who don't have any respect for women?"

"My friends aren't like that."

"Yes, they are, they're all like that. You're mine and you need to listen to what I tell you. I'm the only one you can trust."

If he thought she was going to trust him, he really was insane. He'd tied her to the bed and stripped her out of most of her clothing. Thank God, he'd left her bra and panties on, and double thanks she hadn't worn anything sexy that morning. Only plain cotton.

"If you want me to trust you, then untie me. My wrists hurt and I'm cold."

"Do you think I'm stupid? I know you're stalling. You think he'll come for you. But you can give up on that. You're mine now and for always. When they finally get here, it'll be too late."

She prayed he was wrong. She hadn't had a

lot of faith in her life and had always thought it was ironic it was her name. But she needed to believe, and if there was a chance anyone could save her it would be Chase. He'd find a way to save her from this madman, she believed that with all of her heart.

After trying to reach Faith for the last hour without success, Chase sent a text to Riot. His Spidey-senses were going off, and he didn't like it.

Can't reach Faith, can you check on her?

Will do. Stand by.

He'd gone over to the other side of the base to talk to his old commander since Riot was in Faith's building. He figured it would be safe but ended up there much longer than he expected. His gut told him something was wrong, but it would do him no good to run off half-cocked without knowing for sure.

He'd done some more digging into Iverson. Turned out he didn't even exist before a year ago. Before that Melvin Iverson was a retired tailor in Montana. Witness protection would have given him a new identity, but not someone else's, so it could mean only one thing. Whoever Iverson is or was it wasn't good. Without his fingerprints or DNA, it would be virtually impossible to find out. They'd dusted everything he'd left for Faith and so far, nothing. The man was good, too good.

His cell phone buzzed, and he thought it was Riot. But it was Rock. Before he could reply, the phone rang.

"Boss."

"Yeah. What's up?"

"I think I found out who Iverson was before, and it's not good."

"How did I know you'd say that?"

"Just lucky, I guess? I dunno. I've come up with three other identities. He seems to use them for about a year and then disappears again. We were lucky. Since he thinks he won't get caught, he always uses the doctor persona, and there were photos on file. If not for that we would never have found him."

"Fuck. And Faith was just lucky enough to cross paths with him."

"Apparently. Steele told me about her. Good luck."

"Steele needs to keep his mouth shut about my private life. But thank you. Let me know if you find anything else." Another buzz in his ear interrupted him. "Gotta go. I'll touch base later."

"Riot. Did you find her?"

"Not exactly. She left to meet you over two hours ago."

"What?"

"I didn't ask her to meet me anywhere."

"Exactly."

"Where was she supposed to meet me?"

"According to the petty officer, she went home."

"Dammit."

"We're on our way, meet you there."

"I just heard from Rock. This is not Iverson's first rodeo. I think he's a serial stalker and maybe a serial killer. Watch your six."

"See you there."

Chase prayed the entire drive that he'd get there in time. He should never have left her alone even on base. He'd thought she'd be safe there. But Iverson was smarter than they'd given him credit for, and he'd found a way to get to her. If he harmed a hair on her head, he'd rip him a new one, lots of new ones. Shredding him into a million pieces was too good for him.

Traffic was light, but he felt like he was driving ten miles an hour. Smoke was billowing out from under the front door when he pulled up to her house. Her car was in the driveway. Was he too late?

Charging up to the front door, he pounded on the locked door. Throwing himself at it but it wouldn't budge. He had no idea if Faith was still inside, but he was determined to find out. He circled the house looking for any other way in, he needed to get inside that house and make sure she wasn't there.

"Do you think they're just going to let you get away with this?" Faith was desperate. Time was running out. A million things raced through her mind, most of them about Chase. This madman was going to kill them both if he had his way.

How she wished she'd made different choices, lived more, loved more. Life was too short for not following her heart. Thank God she'd had last night with Chase. This psychotic serial killer might take her life, but he could never take her memories. When he'd confessed to having killed ten women in ten states, she'd known she didn't have a lot of time left.

It wasn't until he told her that she'd been "the one" he'd been searching for all along and now they could spend eternity together, that she really freaked out. She wasn't sure if he was just mad or a psychopath, either way, she was toast.

"Haven't you been listening to me? I told you. This is the end for us. You're my eternity. We're going into the ever after together. It's what I've been working toward for my entire life. No one else was worthy, and I had my doubts about you when I saw you dance. But you're still pure."

"I'm not. Not pure at all. I've been with other men."

"Don't lie to me. I've done my research. You've only been with one man. And that was almost ten years ago. You've been waiting for me, but now it's time for us to go. Your rescuers should have figured it out by now. If I planned this correctly, they'll arrive in time to see you go up in flames." Smoke poured into the room. He'd set the fire while she was passed out. It was getting harder to breathe. They couldn't have much time left.

"No, please. Not fire." Death by fire. Not fire. Anything but fire. Shoot her, stab her, strangle her. But no flames. Please God, no flames.

"It's the final purification for our transcendence. Are you ready to join me in eternity?"

"No. You're insane. You have to let me go. I don't want to go anywhere with you." She was beyond trying to keep him calm, desperation had taken over and she struggled to get free.

He punched her in the jaw. Blood pooled in her mouth where she'd bitten her tongue. She hadn't expected that. But it bought her a few seconds. Over and over in her head she prayed that Chase was on the way. But she wasn't sure he'd get there in time.

He leaned close to her face. "You don't know what you're saying. But after purification, all will be clear." She'd give him purification, and she spit blood into his face. She wasn't going to give up without a fight.

He smiled but didn't bother to wipe away the blood spatter that covered half of his face. "Fight all you want, beloved, nothing will stop us now." Then he pulled out a knife. Had he changed his mind? Was he going to kill her then burn her? As long as she was dead, she'd be okay with that. Burning to death was her greatest fear. He could kill her any other way but that.

He sliced through her panties, and she thought he was going to rape her with the knife. He didn't, but her relief was short-lived. He stabbed over and over again in her stomach, ripping her open.

She screamed as the knife pierced her flesh, and it filled her lungs with smoke. Excruciating pain ripped through her stomach. But all she could do was wheeze and choke on the smoke. Tears trailed down her face as she writhed in pain. The room swam before her eyes, and she tried to focus on Chase, whispering her love for him over and over in her head as she lost consciousness.

CHAPTER 13

Chase burst through the front window and he heard Faith's shriek. The house was filled with thick smoke. Pulling off his shirt, he wrapped it around his nose and mouth and dropped to the floor. Remembering the knives in the kitchen he crawled over and reached for the wooden block and grabbed what he could.

Staying low to the floor, he followed the sound of Faith's screams and tried to block out what it meant. He would get to her in time, he had to. Before he'd burst through the window, he'd dialed nine-one-one. The Fire Department was on the way, and Riot's team couldn't be far behind.

As he made his way down the hallway, he

saw the open door to Faith's bedroom. One, two, three more steps and he'd have her. But the screaming had stopped. Only the hissing and sizzling of the fire could be heard as it consumed everything in its path. He wasn't ready to give up hope, she'd be okay, she had to be. He couldn't lose her again.

The smoke wasn't as bad in the back part of the house, and he could see her outline on the bed through the gray smoke. Iverson was leaning over her with his back to Chase. Why wasn't she fighting? Please God, don't let me be too late.

His SEAL training kicked in and he crept up behind the madman. Before Iverson realized someone was there, Chase sliced the tendons along the back of his legs. He dropped like a stone, unable to hold himself up. It took all of Chase's willpower not to kill him then, but Faith was the only thing that mattered.

Bright red blood poured from the gashes on her stomach. He had to get her out of the house. He couldn't tell the extent of her injuries, but her pulse was barely there. Slicing through the rope that bound her ankles and wrists, he grabbed a piece of her clothing from the floor to apply pressure to the gaping stab wounds.

There was no way he'd make it back through the front door. He had to get her out of there now. Gently placing her back on the bed he begged her to hold on. Then he turned to find something to throw through the window.

"She's mine. You can't have her. The purification has begun." Chase had almost forgotten the lunatic.

"You're wrong. You'll never have her. But you will pay for all that you've done. I'll make sure of that."

"Don't be so sure," Iverson choked out, the smoke making it almost impossible to see beyond the end of his arm. Chase needed to get them out of there.

There weren't a lot of options, and he needed to move quickly. Grabbing the lamp from the nightstand he launched it at the closest window. It cracked the glass but didn't shatter. Fuck it. He made a fist and pressed his knuckles up against the glass. Focusing all his energy on his hand, he pulled back and punched. The window shattered with the force of the blow.

He turned around to grab Faith, but Iverson

had managed to pull her down to the floor and into his lap. Thank God, she was still unconscious, but the blood continued to pour from the wounds on her abdomen.

"Say goodbye. It's time to go." At first, Chase didn't know what he was talking about, then he saw the lighter in Iverson's hand. Their clothing was covered in some type of liquid. Holy shit, he was going to light himself and Faith on fire. He made a dive for the lighter as the flame came to life, but Iverson never had a chance to carry out his plan.

Everything moved in slow motion from that moment. He leaped toward Faith to pull her away as a bullet pierced Iverson's skull. The lighter fell to the floor as Chase pulled Faith from his dead arms.

"We need to get out of here now."

Chase had never been so happy to see anyone as he was to see Riot. He'd saved Faith, and he'd never be able to repay him. Riot grabbed Iverson and followed them through the bedroom window.

The Police and Fire Department vehicles arrived as they cleared the house, and just in time for it to be fully engulfed in flames. A few seconds more and it would have been too late. The EMTs started triage on Faith. The police wanted answers from him but Chase didn't care, there was no way he was leaving her side. Riot spoke to the officer, and he finally relented with the promise that Chase would give his statement at the station. He'd have agree to anything at that point, as long as they didn't keep him from Faith.

Faith never opened her eyes during the trip to the hospital. Chase was terrified he would lose her. There was so much blood everywhere, her face was swollen, and part of her jaw was already turning purple.

Over and over again like a mantra, he whispered, "C'mon, baby, fight, I love you."

Her eyes felt like sandpaper, and she had no idea where she was. Trying again to lift her heavy lids the room came into focus. Where was she? It was bright, too bright. As she lifted her hand to block the light, a sharp pain took her breath away. "That hurts."

"Baby? Do you need something?"

Gingerly turning her head in the direction of the voice, everything hurt. What happened to her?

"Bright. Too bright."

"Okay. Hold on."

The light dimmed, and Faith was able to focus. She tried to talk, but her mouth was so dry. "Water?"

A cup and straw were held to her lips. That helped. Her throat was sore. She wished she could make her mind work.

"Where am I?"

"The hospital. Iverson cut you up pretty badly, and you needed surgery."

Iverson. The name triggered the memories. Tears gathered in her eyes. How had she made it? She'd thought she was dead.

"How long have I been here?" her voice sounded unused and rough.

"Three days. You needed two blood transfusions during surgery. You're going to have to take a break from burlesque for a while."

Her hand went to her stomach, the pain still a bright, painful memory. What had he done to her? "Is he alive?"

"No. I'd like to say I did it, but Riot got him."

She reached for Chase, and as he wrapped his warm hand around hers, she whispered, "I love you."

The next time she opened her eyes Chase was still sitting beside her bed. She didn't know if hours or days had passed but this time her brain was less fuzzy, and the memories were crystal clear.

Lifting the sheet, she looked at her bandaged stomach. It was a miracle he hadn't killed her. So much for praying to be stabbed instead of burned. Who knew that would be the time she'd get her wish.

"Hi, baby."

"Chase. Why are you still here?"

"Where else would I be? You're here, so I'm here."

"You have work to do."

"Don't worry about it, everything is being taken care of. Are you thirsty?"

"Yes." The water cup and straw were lifted to her mouth. Even sucking on the straw hurt.

There was a knock on the door and some

whispering. Then Mick, Max and Riot came in. "How are you, Faith? We've been so worried."

"I'm good. I think. Thank you, Riot. Chase said you helped save me."

"I'm just glad we got there in time."

"Me too." Faith tried to smile but wasn't sure she pulled it off. The pain in her jaw was horrific.

"The others want to visit, but the doctor said only a couple of us could come at a time. You need your rest."

"Tell them I said thank you." Faith wanted to say more, but she was so tired. Without realizing it, she drifted off.

Sometime later she woke, and it was dark. Chase was asleep in the chair next to the bed. She wondered if he'd been there the whole time. The nurse came in and took her vitals. She asked if she could have some water and this time it didn't hurt as much to suck on the straw. Progress.

"What's wrong with me?"

"The doctor will come in a few hours, and he'll explain everything. Can I get you anything else?"

"No, thank you."

"Are you okay, Faith?" She hadn't wanted to wake him, he'd looked so peaceful.

"I don't know. Do you know what's wrong with me?"

"Yes, but only because I told them I was your fiancé, or they wouldn't have let me stay with you. Family only."

"I understand, it's the rules. I follow rules."

"Yes, you do. You're a good girl."

"A lot of good that did me."

"I'm so sorry. I promised to keep you safe, and I failed."

"No, you didn't. I did. I should have known better than to go to the house. Oh God, my house. Is there anything left? I remember smoke."

"We barely got you out before it was immersed in flames."

"It's okay, I didn't want to live there anymore."

"You didn't?"

"No. It's time for a change. Life is too short."

"Yes, it is." Even in the dim light, she saw the confusion on his face. He had no idea what she was trying to say. She was too fuzzy headed to try to put it in different words.

"There's something else. But maybe I should let the doctor tell you."

"No, you tell me. Please." She reached for his hand and noticed that one of them was bandaged. "What happened to your hand?"

"It's nothing. Don't worry about it." He looked so sad, she wondered what else was wrong.

"When Iverson cut you, he did a lot of damage, besides needing blood transfusions, you had to have an emergency hysterectomy."

Hysterectomy. She repeated the word in her head and rolled it around on her tongue. She wouldn't be able to have children, at least not her own. But she was alive. Could she complain? She still had a chance at happiness even if it wasn't the whole package she'd always hoped for. If she could have Chase, they'd figure it out. They could always adopt.

"It's okay."

"I'm sorry, baby. I don't know what else to say."

"Say you love me. Because I love you. And thinking about you was the only thing that kept me alive. I don't want to waste any more of our time. I almost lost you—twice, I can't do that again."

"Are you sure?"

"Yes, but don't make me change my mind."

"Never. I love you, Faith. You will always own my heart."

EPILOGUE

It was six weeks since the fire and Faith's kidnapping. They hadn't taken him alive, but Rock had found fifteen different identities Iverson used over the years. Thankfully, there wouldn't be any more. It hadn't satisfied Rock. He was on a mission to find his real persona, but Chase didn't hold out a lot of hope that he'd be successful.

Checking his watch for the third time, he was surprised his phone hadn't rung yet. They were late. Not a big deal except Faith was the guest of honor. Mick had waited until now to throw a big barbecue for her. Chase could taste the ribs and his stomach growled in response.

"Are you ready, baby?"

After she'd been released from the hospital, Chase took her to the hotel, so she could finish her recovery. He'd been by her side the entire time. His team in Florida had stepped up and ESP was running fine without him there.

"What do you think? Do I look all right?"

He looked up from his phone and his breath caught in his chest. "You're radiant. I'm going to be the envy of every man at the barbecue."

"Don't be silly. They'll all be drooling over Syn and Honey."

"Maybe, but they'll be giving me the side-eye and hoping you dump me." Even though she'd been through hell and still had the traces of bruises on her face, she'd never looked more beautiful.

"Are you sure you haven't been drinking?" She said with a laugh. It was wonderful to hear that sound. He thought he'd lost her, seeing her torn open and all the blood was almost the death of him. And then having to deal with the fact she'd never have children. It surprised him that she had taken the news of the hysterectomy so well. But just because she seemed okay now didn't mean it wouldn't haunt her for years to come. Other than giving her statement to the police, she hadn't talked about any of it, but he hoped one day she would. Everyone had to heal at their own pace.

Over the last few weeks, they had talked about life, her past, their future, and after lots of back and forth, she'd convinced him she wanted to go to Florida. She wanted to start over and leave the memories behind. All she asked is that they'd come visit a few times of year. It was a promise he'd been happy to make.

"Are you ready to go meet your adoring fans?" he asked as he crossed the room and took her into his arms. He'd meant it to be a brief kiss, but as soon as they touched his passion ignited and he didn't stop until they were both breathless.

"I'm sorry. Did I hurt you?"

"I'm not made of glass. How could you hurt me?"

"You're still healing. The doctor…"

"Don't remind me. I feel fine and I'm tired of being careful. I want more kisses like that. More everything."

"I do too, baby. And I'll be happy to make all your dreams come true as soon as the doctor gives his okay. You just have to wait a little longer."

Waiting was hard for both of them and he wanted to give her everything she could wish for and more. Whatever she wanted he'd find a way to give her. She'd taught him so much, but mostly patience. And once she was healed, he planned on teaching her some of his own lessons for the rest of their lives.

ABOUT THE AUTHOR

Lynne St. James is the author of over seventeen books in paranormal, new adult and contemporary romance. She lives in the mostly sunny state of Florida with her husband, an eighty-five-pound, fluffy, Dalmatian-mutt horse-dog, a small Yorkie-poo, and a cat named Pumpkin who rules them all.

When Lynne's not writing stories about second chances and conquering adversity with happily ever afters, you'll find her with a mug of coffee and a crochet hook or a book (or e-reader).

Where to find Lynne:

Email: lynne@lynnestjames.com
Amazon: https://amzn.to/2sgdUTe
BookBub:
https://www.bookbub.com/authors/lynne-st-james
Facebook:

https://www.facebook.com/authorLynneStJames

Website: http://lynnestjames.com

Instagram: https://www.instagram.com/lynnestjames/

Pinterest: https://www.pinterest.com/lynnestjames5

VIP Newsletter sign-up: http://eepurl.com/bT99Fj

Music under the Mistletoe, Book 2.5 – A Raining Chaos Christmas (Novella)

Tempting Flame, Book 3

Anamchara Series

Embracing Her Desires, Book 1

Embracing Her Surrender, Book 2

Embracing Her Love, Book 3

The Vampires of Eternity Series

Twice Bitten Not Shy, Book 1

Twice Bitten to Paradise, Book 2

Twice Bitten and Bewitched, Book 3

Want to be one of the first to learn about Lynne St. James's new releases? Sign up for her newsletter filled with exclusive VIP news and contests!
http://eepurl.com/bT99Fj

Made in the USA
Coppell, TX
26 May 2021

56376196R00114